"Stop fighting me, Leandra, and let me give you the pleasure I know you ache for."

His voice was low and sensual. She felt the fire flickering along her veins, stealing her sanity. She tried to fight it, but she couldn't. The noose of his dark eyes had caught her, and she was helpless.

What was the point of trying to fight him—fight herself? Ever since she had laid eyes on him, Theo Atrides had set a flame alight within her—one she had never known existed, one she could not douse.

She had tried to douse it, dear God, how she had tried! She had tried to hate him, and despise him. She had tried yelling at him and ignoring him. She had wept and she had blushed.

But it was all for nothing. She knew that now.

The dark allure that was Theo Atrides held her in thrall.

Harlequin Presents has an exciting new author....

The Greek Tycoon's Mistress
is the outstanding first novel from Julia James.
It's highly sensual and *very* intense!

Theo Atrides has met his match, and he's decided
he *has* to have Leandra...*whatever* that takes!

They're the men who have everything—
except a bride...

Julia James

THE GREEK TYCOON'S MISTRESS

GREEK
TYCOONS

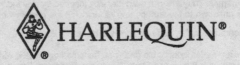

HARLEQUIN®

TORONTO • NEW YORK • LONDON
AMSTERDAM • PARIS • SYDNEY • HAMBURG
STOCKHOLM • ATHENS • TOKYO • MILAN • MADRID
PRAGUE • WARSAW • BUDAPEST • AUCKLAND

ISBN 0-373-12328-0

THE GREEK TYCOON'S MISTRESS

First North American Publication 2003.

Printed in U.S.A.

CHAPTER ONE

THEO ATRIDES narrowed his dark eyes. Fabulously wealthy, dangerous to cross, he was unfairly blessed with a sexual magnetism that had as much to do with the aura of raw power that surrounded him as the physical attributes with which he was so shamelessly endowed.

He paused at the head of the flight of wide-sweeping stairs, looking down into the hotel's crowded banqueting suite. It was a sea of men in black tie, women in rainbow evening dress. Chandeliers caught the glitter of jewels everywhere.

From his vantage point, like an eagle poised in its eyrie, Theo let his alert gaze systematically quarter the throng below, searching with steady purpose. Suddenly he stilled. Beneath the silk-smooth covering of his superbly tailored tuxedo, his tall, powerfully built frame tensed.

Yes, they were there! Both of them.

It was the woman he studied, and as he did so his jaw tightened.

She was dressed to kill. Of that there was no doubt. His expert eye looked her over. Medium height, with a figure both slender and generous—and very, very much on show. Blonde hair cascaded down her bare back in rippling waves. Her skin was pale, like an opalescent pearl against the thigh-length little black dress which dipped so low over the swelling orbs of her breasts that only their delicate tips were veiled by the clinging satin. Likewise, her pert little bottom was tightly, and barely, sheathed, while shimmering stockings covered her legs from exposed thigh to provocative black satin stiletto heels.

A perfect package. So skimpily wrapped. So tempting to unwrap.

She laughed, throwing her head back, letting that fabulous fall of hair ripple down that naked back, exposing the tender line of her throat, the dazzle of diamonds hanging from the succulent morsels of her earlobes.

Theo couldn't even see her face yet, and already he felt his loins tightening. Hardening.

The rush of sensual pleasure of his own ultra-masculine reaction warred with a hard, tight shaft, not of desire, but anger, mingling explosively. Women like that were trouble. Especially for the men they caught in their toils.

He should know...

Slowly, he began to walk down the wide sweep of stairs.

Leandra had never felt more naked in her life. With every breath she feared that her breasts would finally escape her low-cut bodice completely, and every movement of her legs would make the tight sheath of her skirt ride up over her bottom. Chris must have been mad to make her wear a dress like this!

But he had been adamant that she should look as brazenly sexy as she could, or there was no point in any of this charade at all.

Even so, she hated the way she looked in the tarty get-up!

She took a quick but deep, controlled breath—the same technique she used to subdue stage fright. For that was all this was, Leandra reminded herself—a stage performance. Certainly a glitzy charity gala at one of London's top hotels was not her customary stamping ground.

She was more used to pub theatres and grimy green rooms—the usual lot of a struggling actress. Now, thanks to Chris, she was standing beside a handsome young Greek millionaire—and almost sick with nerves.

Demos Atrides, who ran the UK subsidiary of the vast Atrides business empire, turned to her with a reassuring smile. She gave him a wide smile back, the way her role demanded.

She liked him a lot, and not just because of Chris. For all

his wealth Demos was very diffident—he needed Chris's buoyant confidence to keep his spirits up, Leandra knew. She wasn't the only one dreading the coming confrontation.

Would their charade be convincing? Leandra swallowed. She mustn't be the one to let them down—after all, she *was* the professional actress.

Demos's light touch on her arm made her start slightly.

'He's here,' he said in his soft, mellifluous voice, the Greek accent distinct. As was the tension in his face.

Leandra drew in her breath. 'Here goes,' she said, and wished herself luck.

As he approached them Theo Atrides felt his mood darken. He didn't want to be here, but his grandfather Milo had insisted. As patriarch of the Atrides clan he was used to getting his own way. That was why, Theo knew, Milo was taking it so hard that his younger grandson refused to come to heel.

Not that it was like Demos to cause trouble. He'd always done everything Theo had asked of him, running the London office diligently and competently. His affairs had always been conducted with discretion; even Theo knew nothing about them.

Why make such a fuss about this one?

Theo's mouth thinned. The reason was right in front of him. Blonde, lush and very, very sexy. No wonder his little cousin didn't want to come home and marry Sofia Allessandros, the bride Milo had chosen for him. What man would want to give up a mistress like this?

Demos Atrides felt the heavy hand on his shoulder, and for a moment it felt like the clap of doom. Then he recovered.

'Theo!' he exclaimed, with a forced expression of delight. 'It's good to see you. My PA told me you'd phoned from the jet to ask where I'd be tonight.' He glanced beyond his cousin. 'Where is Milo?'

'Resting,' returned his cousin tersely. 'The flight was a strain. You shouldn't have made it necessary, Demos.'

The words were a reproof, and Demos coloured slightly.

'There was no need for him to come,' he replied defensively.

'Wasn't there?'

Deliberately Theo shifted his focus to the woman hanging on to Demos's arm like a gilded limpet. As his eyes lit full on her face for the first time he felt, like an electric shock, a response that was like a kick in the gut.

For a moment his brain churned. She wasn't in the least what he'd been expecting from what he'd seen of her so far. He'd assumed that the brazenly sexy body would be accompanied by nothing more than a vacuous expression and an avaricious nature.

Instead, a pair of intelligent amber-coloured eyes flashed up at him, deep-set and lustrous, catching him with an unexpected beauty despite being caked in eyeshadow and their lashes clotted with too much mascara. Something showed in their depths, but before his scrambled brain could identify it it was gone. Theo dismissed it, and went on studying the rest of her face. It was layered in make-up, far too much of it, but the excess could not camouflage the height of her cheekbones and the fine, straight line of her nose. Nor could the sticky scarlet lipstick disguise the tender curve of her mouth.

Theo suddenly felt an odd desire to take a tissue and sweep away the acres of gunk smeared all over her extraordinary natural beauty...

For a moment, the merest instant, something stirred in him that had nothing to do with his immediate and all too easily identifiable reaction to the lush physical charms of the woman in front of him. Something that disturbed him—moved him...

He snapped his mind away. It didn't matter an iota what he thought of Demos's mistress. It only mattered that he got his cousin away from her and back to Athens and his engagement to Sofia Allessandros.

It was what everyone expected—especially Milo. He was

desperate to see the next Atrides generation secure. He had never, Theo knew, recovered from the tragedy that had almost overwhelmed the family eight years ago, when both his sons and their wives had been killed when the Atrides jet had crashed. Theo himself had hardly had time to grieve. At the age of twenty-four he had found himself single-handedly in charge of the entire Atrides business empire as Milo suffered a near-fatal stroke at the loss of his sons. Business rivals, seeing the Atrides clan so stricken, had swooped.

Theo had fought them off, swiftly becoming battle hardened, and now, at thirty-two, the Atrides empire was stronger and wealthier than ever. No one dared challenge its ruthless boss these days.

All it needed now was a new heir for the next generation—Milo was right.

But it would not be Theo who provided one.

Marriage was not for Theo. Never would be.

If anyone was going to give Milo the great-grandsons he craved, it would have to be Demos—and Sofia Allessandros. As for the foxy piece clinging to Demos's arm—well, she'd just have to look for another rich lover!

His eyes swept over her again. With looks like that it shouldn't take her long to find one…

Leandra stared at the man looking her over with those dark, heavy-lidded eyes. Just stared. Oh, good grief, but he was devastating! Absolutely devastating! She'd heard enough about Big Bad Cousin Theo from Demos, heaven knew. He wasn't just a tough, ruthless businessman.

Women flocked around Theo Atrides, and he helped himself to the ones he wanted, sampled them, then discarded them for fresh sweetmeats. Leandra could see why—and it was not, definitely not, just because he was stinking rich. Theo Atrides could have pulled women by the bucketload without a drachma to his name!

Leandra felt herself helpless under the impact of his sheer physical presence, from the commanding height of his six-foot-plus frame to the subtle but heady scent of his aftershave mingled with raw, potent maleness. The photos she'd seen of him—family shots in Demos's apartment, glossy spreads in celebrity magazines—whilst capturing his eye-catching good looks, had not prepared her for the real Theo Atrides. Let alone for his effect on her.

She'd blithely assumed, because she was totally unattracted by Demos's looks, that she'd be as immune to his cousin's.

Oh, boy, what a mistake! Theo Atrides's features were much stronger, his eyes keen and hooded, darker than his twenty-six-year-old cousin's and far, far more knowing. His nose was a strong slash, his cheekbones powerful and high, and his jaw might have been hewn with a chisel. His mouth had none of Demos's fullness, but was wide and mobile and, Leandra registered with a hollow feeling, a million times sexier...

In fact, in just about every atom of his being, Theo Atrides was a million times sexier than his cousin.

And a million times more dangerous. In an act of unconscious self-preservation Leandra veiled her assessing eyes, adopting instead the vacuous expression of a bimbo that fitted the charade she was acting out. Doing so had its compensations. It allowed her to look him over just the way she wanted to—needed to.

Not that he'd look twice at her. All his women, however briefly they lasted, were either celebrities in their own right— a couple of supermodels, an opera singer and an Oscar-winning movie star sprang effortlessly to mind—or else they were blue-blooded scions of Europe's cosmopolitan aristocracy and America's Wall Street plutocrats.

Except that he *was* looking at her. Theo Atrides was looking her over very, very thoroughly, with all the expertise of a practised connoisseur of the very best in female beauty.

It was a nerve-tingling experience.

As she felt, almost physically, those dark, knowing eyes wash over her, Leandra could feel her legs jellify. Her breath had frozen solid in her throat, making it impossible to breathe. Her heart, it seemed, slewed to a stop in her chest and her eyes were stretched so wide she must be goggling. Then, just as she started to go into complete meltdown under his blatantly sexual appraisal, she realised she could see contempt openly sitting in his eyes. It was obvious what he thought of a woman dressed as revealingly as she was.

Two impulses warred within her. One was to grab the nearest tablecloth and cover herself up. The other was to slap his face so hard it would spin the stars for him!

Of course she did neither—she could not afford to.

Instead, she behaved in the way that her role in this elaborate charade required her to behave. Badly.

'Demos,' she husked, pressing into his side more closely, unconsciously seeking his protection from such an arrant sexual predator, 'who is this gorgeous, gorgeous man?'

Leandra's voice was slightly breathy. It was not entirely put on. Her body was out of control, reacting to this man's presence in ways she had only ever read about, never experienced. It was a mix of terrifying and exhilarating.

Demos opened his mouth to answer, but was forestalled.

'Theo Atrides,' murmured his cousin. His voice had dropped a register and taken on a deep, dark husk of its own, heavy with his drawling Greek accent. The raw sexiness of it made Leandra's toes curl, accompanied as it was by a kilowatt's worth of sexual charge blazing through eyes which were suddenly, devastatingly, heavy-lidded and half closed.

He turned to Demos.

'And this is...?' He paused expectantly, the purring note still deep in his voice.

His appeal to his cousin sent a frisson of waspish anger through Leandra. Doesn't he think me capable of answering for myself? she thought indignantly.

'Leandra,' supplied Demos. He said her name reluctantly.

'Ross—' completed Leandra, with the very slightest bite to her voice.

'Leandra,' echoed Theo Atrides drawlingly, ignoring the

irrelevance of her surname. Women like her had no need of anything other than a first name—preferably something exotic.

'You are very lovely, Leandra.' He paused infinitesimally. 'Very lovely. All over.'

The heavy-lidded dark eyes washed over her. She felt they were stripping off every last vestige of clothing. Then he helped himself to her hand.

His touch was as electric as his look. To her shame, Leandra believed that she actually trembled as he made contact.

His hand was large and smooth. Warm and strong. And very powerful. Hers looked pale and fragile within its olive-tanned grasp.

Leisurely, Theo lifted her scarlet-tipped, freshly manicured fingers to his lips. But instead of grazing her knuckles in a courtly fashion, as Leandra was steeling herself to expect, he turned her hand over to expose her palm and bent his head.

As his lips touched her flesh she felt them part slightly. Then, in a caress that exploded every nerve-ending in her palm, they laved her skin softly and sensuously. She felt a prickle of arousal all over her body, delicious and enticing. Warm, liquid coils of heat pooled in her veins. Then suddenly, shockingly, she felt the tip of his tongue flicker exploringly at the junctions of her fingers.

Shock, outrage and a sizzle of raw sexual excitement electrified her, searing the breath in her fractured lungs. She couldn't move even as he released her from his shockingly intimate caress.

She grabbed her hand back into her own possession. It felt as if every nerve-ending in it had been set on fire, humming like flame racing along her veins. For one long, overwhelming moment she felt as if the world was whirling round her, and the only still point was the flare of sensation echoing in her hand.

Her lips parted and she stared, helplessly, at Theo Atrides.

He smiled down at her. A warm, intimate smile. A knowing, indulgent smile. A dangerous, sexy smile.

Almost, almost she felt herself moving blindly towards him, to press herself up against his lean, hard body and give herself to him absolutely. He was like a powerful magnet sucking her towards him.

But she had to resist. She must! She was here to play his cousin's mistress—nothing more. Forcibly she relaxed her muscles, and by sheer effort of will—still reeling from the sensual onslaught of Theo Atrides's terrifyingly skilful, insolent mouth on her exposed, defenceless skin—she managed to pull her body back from leaning into his.

Thee mou, thought Theo, as she drew back with obvious reluctance, the girl couldn't have come on stronger if she'd given him her telephone number! She'd all but gone up in flames for him! What the hell would she be like if he got her horizontal?

A sudden, overpowering image of her lying beneath him, naked and aching for him, yielding her body to him with soft moans, filled his mind with devastating, vivid clarity. He thrust it aside brutally. This was no time to get the hots for a woman who was threatening the stability of his family and its very future! All her sizzling reaction to his deliberate sexual provocation had proved was that, whatever she felt for Demos, it wasn't anything that stopped her lighting up for any other man. The faithful type she wasn't!

He turned back to his cousin.

As his attention snapped off Leandra wondered why she felt bereft, instead of relieved—as if a source of heat suddenly turned off had revealed how cold she had been feeling.

All her life.

In a daze she tried to make herself concentrate on what Theo was saying to his cousin. It was hard, because her brain felt like mush.

'So,' Theo said to Demos, his deep voice sounding amused, 'this is what is keeping you in London so long, I see! I can't say I'm surprised, now I've met this delicious morsel of female flesh—' His eyes worked over Leandra once more, so brazenly she felt her stomach drop even as anger leapt in her throat at such a description. 'But,' he went on, holding up a hand peremptorily and focusing back on his cousin, 'all good things come to an end, Demos. Sofia is waiting for you. It's time to come home.'

Leandra could feel Demos tense.

'I'm not ready,' he replied tersely. His usually mild voice sounded strained.

'Then *be* ready,' said Theo unforgivingly. He reached out and closed his hand around his cousin's shoulder, turning him slightly away from Leandra as if she were an intruder on the scene.

He switched to Greek, reinforcing her exclusion.

'Milo's on the way out, Demos. It's only a matter of time. His doctors know it and he knows it. He's old—he's had too much to bear in his life—don't do this to him. Come home and get engaged to Sofia. It's all he asks. He needs to know that the next generation is assured—you can't blame him for being anxious. He knows, *Christos,* he knows, just how uncertain life is! He needs to know that a great-grandson could be on the way soon—he needs an heir.'

He spoke rapidly, in a low voice.

Stiffly, Demos answered. 'Milo has two grandsons, Theo. Why don't you oblige?'

Theo's jaw tightened. 'I'm not the marrying kind, little cousin.'

For a second something showed in Demos's eyes.

'And suppose I'm not either?' he said.

There was something in Demos's voice that stayed his cousin. Theo looked at him narrowly.

'What's that supposed to mean?' he asked slowly.

For a long moment Demos just looked across at him, as if he was going to say something. Then, with a fling of his hand, he shook Theo off his shoulder.

'It means I'm having too much fun to want to settle down!

I'm not ready to marry anyone, let alone Sofia Allessandros!' An urgent note entered his voice. 'Make Milo see that, Theo. Make him!'

Anger lashed through Theo. Anger at both of them—Milo for wanting to arrange other people's lives because he was taking leave of his own, and Demos for insisting on living his own life when he had responsibilities to meet!

And most of all anger, irrational but powerful, against the girl plastered against Demos—the cause of all this trouble.

He wanted out of this! He hadn't wanted to come here, and now he was here he wanted to wash his hands of the whole business. He wanted to get away—away from the endless demands of family, of business—go some place where all he had to do was gaze out over the blue Aegean, hear the cicadas calling, inhale the heady scent of the maquis, feel the zephyred wind from the south on his body.

With a soft, compliant woman in his arms...

Like the one at Demos's side...

He gave a rasp in his throat, banishing the dangerously enticing vision.

'Enough!' His hand slashed the air with a short, brusque slash. 'I'll expect you tomorrow, Demos. Milo wants to see you at nine. We're in the penthouse suite here. Be on time.' He eyed his cousin darkly, his harsh gaze sweeping out to Leandra. 'And get some sleep tonight!' he finished, reverting to English.

His eyes flickered briefly over her face. The expression in them made her want to hit him. His thoughts were naked. With a woman like her at his side what man would want to sleep?

He, for one, could think of a thousand better things to do with her—

He snapped his mind away again. The woman was an irrelevance.

Soon her brief intrusion into his family affairs would be over—permanently.

*   *   *

Demos Atrides opened the door to his apartment and ushered Leandra inside. Immediately she was tightly enveloped in a bear hug.

'Well,' demanded the extremely handsome blond embracing her with long familiarity. 'How did it go? Did he show?'

Leandra extricated herself, tossing her evening bag on the silk-covered sofa, and kicked off one of her high heels. Her feet were killing her. She said nothing. She didn't think she could for the moment.

'Oh, yes, he showed all right,' said Demos behind her. His voice was tight.

'And?' demanded the other young man. 'Did he fall for it?'

Demos gave a short laugh, displaying the tension he was still under.

'Hook, line and sinker—isn't that what you say?'

The blond laughed, showing an expanse of gleaming white teeth in a brilliant smile that lit his handsome face. Leandra laughed too, but hers was short, with an edge to it.

'With the emphasis on hook—as in hooker,' she said bitingly. 'God, Chris.' She kicked off her other shoe and flexed her aching ankles. 'Thanks to that dress you poured me into, Theo Atrides looked at me like I was some kind of tart!'

A shiver went through her at the memory of the way Demos's cousin had looked her over—and more than looked...

But Chris was not dismayed. 'That's brilliant, Lea—just what we wanted! He's got to think Demos is totally captivated by his sexy little mistress! Speaking of sexy—' he caught her shoulders '—you, darling, look absolutely edible! Yum, yum!'

Leandra was in no mood for his foolery. Reaction and revulsion were setting in with a vengeance.

'Leave off, Chris!' she said, pushing his hands off her shoulders and heading towards the bathroom. 'I need to get out of this ridiculous costume!'

*   *   *

The evening had been far more of an ordeal than she had thought it would be—thanks to that wretched dress and Theo Atrides! She stepped out of the shower and towelled herself vigorously. It had seemed so easy, as well as a good deed, to pretend to be Demos's mistress. All she'd had to do was move into the spare bedroom in Demos's luxury apartment and spend the last three weeks appearing to be living with him—until his family finally got the message that he wasn't coming home to marry Sofia Allessandros.

Leandra stared at her reflection as she combed out the knots in her wet hair, her face set. Had tonight's performance been sufficiently convincing? Would the Atrideses finally leave him in peace now?

She hoped so—with a shudder she knew she couldn't face another encounter with Theo Atrides. Her nerves couldn't stand it.

A sudden shaft of depression hit her. Theo Atrides was the most incredibly attractive male she'd ever laid eyes on, and he'd seen her as nothing more than a sexy, trashy tart.

But what if he hadn't?

Her comb paused and her imagination took flight. She saw herself, gowned in black still, but soft velvet, long, sweeping the ground, its modest *décolletage* set with a single white rose, her hair caught in a low, elegant chignon at the nape of her neck, her make-up subtle, her perfume elusive…

If Theo Atrides had seen her looking like that then perhaps those heavy-lidded eyes would have gazed at her quite differently, mused Leandra dreamily. Sensually, yes, but without that offensive glint of contempt he hadn't bothered to hide. His eyes would have shown nothing but the desire of man for woman. As old as time. An eternal hunger yearning to be sated.

She sighed, beguiled by her own impossible vision. Then, abruptly, she sobered. Struggling actresses, whatever they wore, were not his fare. And even if they were, she added crushingly, it wouldn't do you any good! Even filmstar Madeleine Fareham with her precious Oscar hadn't gone the distance! The papers were full of her marrying her latest co-star on the rebound from Theo Atrides!

Decisively, Leandra tugged the last of the knots from her newly washed hair as if she were tugging something out of her that had just taken root—a weed that looked like an orchid but was really nothing more than poison ivy.

Back in the lounge, Chris and Demos were drinking coffee. Leandra, swathed in a towelling robe, poured herself a cup and collapsed next to Chris. He put his arm around her shoulder.

'Better now?' he asked sympathetically.

She nodded. 'Yes. Sorry—but, honestly, the way you dressed me up—I just felt so exposed! And Demos's cousin looked at me like I was some kind of total floozie! It was horrible! Still…' she took a deep breath '…it's all over now. Thank goodness. Oh, Demos.' She leant forward and tossed the diamond earrings in his lap. 'Here you go.'

He caught them and put them on the coffee table. Then he met Leandra's eyes.

'Lea—thank you. Thank you a thousand times.' He sounded embarrassed. 'And I am sorry that my cousin behaved towards you in such a disrespectful way.'

Leandra held up a hand. She didn't want Demos feeling bad about it.

'It's OK,' she said lightly, playing it down. 'I'll survive. And, hey, it's like Chris says—that was the whole plan—to make me look like a rich man's sex toy. I should be glad he believed it!'

She looked down into her coffee cup. Oh, Theo Atrides had believed she was a sex toy all right! Memory leapt at her, searing her belly with its heat as she felt again the echo of his hand taking hers, kissing her palm…the touch of his flickering tongue…

Beneath the protectively thick towelling robe she could feel her breasts tighten.

Angry mortification filled her. She could tell herself all she liked that it had been hateful to be treated like that, but she knew she was a liar.

Theo Atrides had had an effect on her that she had never encountered in her life before. It had overwhelmed her, blasted her out of the sky like a fireball...

She'd been helpless, totally helpless. If he'd wanted, he could have taken her hand and led her away from Demos—led her away to a private room and folded her against his body, lowered that hard, mobile mouth to hers and done anything he wanted to her...anything at all...

She stared down into her coffee, appalled by this shaming realisation.

A shudder went through her as she fought to throw his image, his memory, out of her mind.

'Lea—are you all right?'

She jerked her head up. 'I'm fine—fine. Just tired, that's all.'

Chris was looking at her closely.

'Did the bastard get to you, Lea?' he asked quietly. At his side Demos stiffened at this cavalier description of the cousin he had always looked up to, but he said nothing.

Leandra bit her lip. She could deny the way she'd reacted to Theo Atrides, but it wouldn't fool either of them for long. She might as well admit it now.

'Yes,' she acknowledged. 'But it doesn't matter—all that matters is that he leaves Demos alone now.'

She made her voice bright and cheerful and decided she had to just pull herself together. It didn't matter a jot that she had all but melted over Theo Atrides. It didn't matter that he was the most devastating male she had ever seen. It didn't even matter that he thought her nothing but a wind-up sex toy.

She would never set eyes on him again.

Theo Atrides had come and gone in her life. He wouldn't be back.

CHAPTER TWO

THEO stared moodily out over Hyde Park from the penthouse suite where he and his grandfather were staying. The trees had turned autumnal already; summer was over.

His mood was grim. Demos had just left, and the exchange with Milo had not been pleasant. When his grandfather had finished lecturing him on duty, responsibility, family and Sofia Allessandros waiting in Athens for him to deign to turn up, Demos had stubbornly repeated what he'd said to Theo the night before. He wasn't ready to get married. That was all. He was enjoying his bachelor life.

Then he'd walked out.

Theo turned back towards Milo.

'You are so sure of this marriage?' he heard himself ask.

Milo flashed him a dark look from eyes which, though wrinkled, were still keen and sharp.

'Demos needs a good marriage. Sofia Allessandros is just the girl for him.'

Theo paused. 'I know,' he said carefully, 'that you are in a hurry. But can't you give him more time? It's *his* life, Milo.'

The dark, shrewd eyes stared at him.

'I'm worried about him,' he said. 'I want to see him safe with Sofia Allessandros.'

There seemed to be meaning in his words. Theo frowned.

'This woman of his? A pillow-friend, nothing more. He won't marry her, if that's what's worrying you!'

The dark eyes snapped and Milo's mouth thinned.

'Young men are foolish!' He fixed Theo with a piercing, uncomfortable look. 'You would have made such a foolish marriage...'

The accusation hung in the air. For a moment Theo stilled. Then, with a deliberate shrug of his powerful shoulders, he said, 'Well, you and my father soon sorted that out, didn't you? And that other ''minor complication'' it involved!'

The accusation had been returned, and Milo felt it. His eyes snapped again. 'Don't take that tone! We did what was necessary. A woman like that—you should be grateful!'

Theo stilled again. 'Grateful.' The word fell heavily from his lips.

A harsh, impatient rasp sounded in the old man's throat. 'Money showed her true colours! It always does with women of her stamp!'

He shifted restlessly in the chair he was sitting in. Pain flickered briefly in his face. Theo saw it. Pity filled him. The past was gone—his grandfather and his father had done what they had thought best, by their lights. And they had been right, he knew. Money did show true colours. And he was grateful, just as Milo said he should be. Grateful to have had his illusions shattered.

Illusions were always dangerous. In business, and in bed.

Theo had no illusions any more. Never again. He knew what he wanted from women now. It was simple, pleasurable—and painless. As for taking a wife—no. No matter how much Milo pressurised him to continue the family name, he knew he would never trust a woman with his happiness again.

'Sofia will make Demos a good wife. You know that.'

Milo's voice brought him back to the problem in hand.

Yes, Sofia Allessandros would make Demos a good wife. She had been groomed from childhood to be the perfect wife for a rich man. And, like every well brought up Greek girl, she was as untouched as the morning dew.

Theo's brow darkened briefly. The image of Demos's lovely young pillow-friend slid into his mind, lush and enticing. Tempting men from their duties, their responsibilities—their families.

As if reading his thoughts, Milo spoke again.

'Demos won't look twice at Sofia while he's got a mistress to warm his bed.'

The grim look returned to Theo's face. Leandra's lush body swayed in his vision.

'That one would warm any man's bed!'

His grandfather's eyes narrowed. 'Yours, Theo?'

Theo gave a rasp of denial. But Milo hadn't built a business empire from scratch without being able to read men's thoughts. He gave a sudden rough laugh.

'Well, that would be one way of removing the obstacle!'

Theo's mouth set in a thin line.

'I was thinking of something a little more basic.'

His grandfather gave that rough laugh again. In his time, Milo Atrides had kept mistresses by the score.

'Nothing is more basic than sex,' he said bluntly.

'Except money,' corrected his grandson. He looked straight at Milo. 'That method never fails. You, of all people, should know that.'

If his grandfather heard the bitterness in his grandson's voice, he ignored it. He had done what he had had to do. The woman had been a danger to his family. As this one now was.

'Yes,' he agreed, relaxing back in his chair. 'Money's a good method.'

Theo nodded.

'I'll take care of it. She'll be out of his bed in a week!'

Leandra frowned in concentration. 'Can you just give me my cue again please, Demos?'

'Of course.'

He smiled obligingly, but Leandra could see that his eyes were troubled. The morning's interview with his grandfather had been painful, she knew. She felt so sorry for him. In the weeks she'd spent at his apartment she'd grown to like this young man who came from such a totally different world. Their only link was Chris. Why did his family keep trying to arrange his life for him? It was bad enough his grandfather pressurising him to marry—now even his cousin was joining in!

His cousin was totally unlike Demos, she mused. With Demos she felt safe and comfortable. With Theo Atrides she'd never feel safe or comfortable. She gave an inward shiver.

Then, resolutely, she turned back to the page. Demos was kindness itself in agreeing to help her learn this fiendishly difficult part. It would bring neither fame nor fortune, but it was a privilege to have been chosen for it. The Marchester Festival, highly specialised though it was, had an excellent reputation. Besides, the effort of learning it helped to take her mind off Theo Atrides.

And she needed all the help she could get. He was haunting her. She couldn't get him out of her mind. His hooded eyes were vivid in her brain, looking her over—setting her body on fire...

He intruded everywhere, even in her dreams. Which was ridiculous—she would never see him again. He'd go back to Athens with his grandfather, admit defeat over Demos, and that would be that.

He would admit defeat, wouldn't he? After all, in the end there was nothing either Theo or his grandfather could do to force Demos to marry Sofia Allessandros. All Demos had to do was stand firm.

Would Sofia mind being rejected by the man she was expecting to marry? No one seemed too concerned about *her* wishes in all of this!

'Demos,' she heard herself asking, 'are you sure Sofia won't be upset that you won't marry her? It sounds like she's spent her whole life assuming you will.'

He looked away uncomfortably. 'I can't help it, Leandra. You know I can't marry her. For me to do so would be to wrong her grievously.'

She bit her lip. Carefully, she said, 'Can't you tell her why? And your family?'

Demos's face shuttered. 'Do not ask that of me,' he answered. There was anguish in his voice, and guilt—Leandra could not press him. He had burdens of his own to carry. One day he would be able to set them down, but not now, she knew. He was not ready.

Instead, she asked another question.

'Demos, when is your grandfather likely to go back to Athens?'

The shadowed look in his eyes intensified.

'I am not sure,' he admitted. 'Theo wants him to see a Harley Street specialist while he is in London.'

'Oh. Then what would you like me to do? What would be best?'

'If you would be kind enough to stay here I would be most grateful, Leandra.' There was entreaty in Demos's voice.

She smiled reassuringly. 'Of course, if that is what you want. I can hardly complain about the standard of my accommodation! I'm in the lap of luxury here! And I'm happy to help out if there's anything I can do. There's a saying in English—in for a penny, in for a pound!' She tapped at the page of her script with a grin. 'But I'll drive a hard bargain, my young Greek millionaire! Back to work!'

He pored over the words with her, heads together. Suddenly she gave a laugh. Her amber eyes gleamed wickedly.

'Oh, if your cousin could see us now! He'd never believe it! Never!'

Remembering the look of unveiled contempt in Theo Atrides's eyes as he looked her over like a piece of sextrash, she felt a sharp sense of satisfaction.

It was a beautiful day, even for central London. The mild, sunny autumn weather was still holding. Leandra swung down the Edgware Road, her body pleasantly tired and stretched from her dance class in Paddington. Acting was hard work. London heaved with struggling actresses, and competition for parts was fierce. Still, acting was what she had always wanted to do, and her very staid parents had been happy enough for her to work it out of her system—as they'd been sure she would within a few years.

Her eyes shadowed, grief showing in them briefly. Their death in a coach crash on holiday had been so sudden, so brutal. Even now, nearly two years later, the memory was like a knife in her breast.

Chris had been so kind to her, proving a true friend, taking her under his wing and looking after her while she was raw with grief and shock. No wonder she hadn't hesitated when he had asked her for a favour for Demos.

The blare of a car horn made her jump. The Edgware Road was clogged with traffic, and she was still quite some way from Demos's Mayfair apartment. She made an inward grimace. She would miss that fabulous apartment all right! Going back to her tiny studio flat on a noisy road south of the Thames—all she could afford at London property prices, even with the legacy from her parents—was not something she was looking forward to. For the first time she could understand why women would agree to exchange their self-respect for such a luxurious lifestyle.

Her amber eyes darkened. That was exactly the kind of woman Theo Atrides thought her—that much was obvious. The kind who latched on to men just because they were rich! Not for the first time she felt a stab of anger at him. Oh, she would love to see him eat his words! 'Delicious morsel of female flesh' indeed!

She should not have recalled them to mind. For with them came an image of the man saying them—tall, powerful, those dark, heavy-lidded eyes making her stomach flip over slowly, oh, so slowly as her legs turned to jelly...

Someone brushed past her on the crowded pavement. Automatically she moved to one side, and then, just at the same time, someone brushed her from that side as well. She glanced either way, frowning suddenly. London was safe enough on the whole, if you were sensible, but muggings happened all the time. She clutched at her shoulder bag more tightly, but even as she did so she felt her body crowded from both sides.

It happened so quickly. One moment she was being hustled on the wide pavement and the next, in broad daylight, on a busy London road, two men had caught her by either elbow, pulled her forward and then, before she could scream, she was being thrust into the gaping interior of a huge black-windowed limousine that was suddenly there, pulled up at the kerb. The door slammed behind her. Her head was tilted forcibly back, a pad pressed over her nose and mouth. Her eyes flared in terror and then, as the drug sucked into her gasping lungs, fluttered helplessly shut as consciousness drained away.

'Well, did he tell you how long I've got?'

Milo's voice was harsh, but Theo could hear the exhaustion in it. Milo was tough, but age was finally taking its toll.

'Six, maybe nine months. A year if you are spectacularly fortunate.'

Theo did not mince his words. He would not be thanked if he did.

Milo's eyes gleamed fiercely. 'Hah! Long enough to see a great-grandson on the way!'

Theo looked out of the window of the chauffeur-driven limo. They were nosing down Harley Street. Traffic was bad. Rush hour was all around them.

He did not answer his grandfather. Instead, he said, 'He wants to put you on a different drug regime. Says it could buy you time. He wants to start you straight away, but he'll need to monitor you for a week or two to see how you respond. You don't need to be in hospital. So I've taken the suite for another fortnight. I'll stay with you, naturally.'

His grandfather gave a rasp. 'Not in that damned hotel, you won't! And neither will I. We'll stay at the apartment. I want to see more of Demos anyway!'

Theo frowned. 'The girl is still there. I haven't had a chance to buy her off yet!'

Milo gave a harsh laugh.

'Save your money. She's been dealt with.'

Theo's head swivelled.

'I said I'd handle it—'

'Well, I've saved you the trouble. And my way was a whole lot cheaper! And more certain.'

'What do you mean?' Theo's words were slow, filled with foreboding. 'What have you done?'

Milo looked at his grandson with grim satisfaction.

'She's gone,' he said. 'She was in the way, so I had her removed.'

Cold snaked down Theo's spine.

'What…exactly…have you done with her?'

Milo gave another harsh bark of laughter.

'Don't look at me as if I'd had her murdered! She's perfectly safe. Sunning herself on a beach.'

Theo's brows drew together.

'She agreed to go on holiday?' He sounded sceptical.

'I didn't waste time asking her. I just sent her!'

The cold snaked down Theo's spine again.

'You *sent* her? How? Where?'

'How? I had her picked up and packed off. I had a tail put on her when she left Demos's apartment this morning. She was put in a car, kept quiet, driven to an airfield and that was that. Don't look at me like that, boy! I'm not incapable yet! I know agencies who will do such things and be discreet about it!'

But his grandson was staring at him with an appalled look on his face.

'Are you telling me,' he said, his voice hollow, 'that you had her abducted?'

Milo made a testy noise in his throat. 'I had her removed! That's all! She's perfectly safe—I told you!'

A word escaped Theo that was not in polite usage.

'*Where?*' he demanded urgently. 'Where is she, Milo?'

His grandfather gave his harsh laugh again.

'So eager to find her?' he jeered. 'Maybe you do want to replace Demos between her legs!'

Theo ignored the crude jibe. The cold had spread from his spine through every part of his body. Had Milo gone insane? Had he really had a British citizen abducted from the streets of London and flown out of the country?

'Where is she?'

Milo's eyes flashed. 'Don't take that tone with me! She's on that hideaway island of yours. The one you take your own pillow-friends to!'

Theo's eyes stabbed black fire.

'What?'

Milo gave another snort. 'Hah, did you think I did not know of the place? Of course I knew! But if you want to keep a place like that to yourself, who am I to interfere? A man wants to be private when he communes with Eros. I respect that. So you see—' he sounded well pleased with himself '—Demos's little tart will be perfectly at home there. She can improve her tan and pretty herself up for her next protector. And by the time I let her off the island Demos and Sofia will be engaged!'

He cast a triumphant look at his grandson, still staring at him appalled.

'Cheaper than a pay-off, and far more certain.'

'With only one slight downside.' Theo's voice was hollow. 'Abduction is a criminal offence.'

How Theo got through the next twenty-four hours he didn't afterwards remember. Milo, utterly oblivious of what he had done, had had to be taken back to the hotel. Then Theo had to confront a frantic Demos who had realised, when he returned to his apartment from his office, that Leandra seemed to have disappeared off the face of the earth.

'Milo did *what*?'

Demos had gone white.

'She's safe, Demos. That much is clear.' Theo spoke tersely.

'I'm going out there right away!'

Theo caught his shoulder. 'No! I will deal with it.'

Demos glared at him accusingly. Theo could read his thoughts. He shook his head. His smile was grim. 'Even I have my limits, little cousin.' For a moment they looked into each other's eyes. Theo had been like a big brother to Demos all his life.

'Trust me,' said Theo, holding his cousin's stricken gaze. 'You stay here and take care of Milo. Right now—' he inhaled sharply '—I don't want to be too close to him!' He shook his head. 'I knew he was desperate, but to commit such an act! He seems to have absolutely no idea of what he's done!'

Grimly, Theo knew that if he couldn't find a way to silence the girl she might drag the Atrides name through the criminal courts. Milo could even be facing a jail sentence.

As for what the press would make of it...

He snapped his mind away. His hand squeezed on Demos's shoulder.

'Trust me,' he said again, and took his leave.

But even then his problems hadn't been over. The Atrides jet had been stranded on the tarmac. UK airspace had been in chaos—the air traffic control system had gone down again. It wasn't until well into the next day that Theo had finally been able to get airborne.

Then, when he'd landed in Athens, he'd found Sofia's father, Yannakis Allessandros, had heard the Atrides jet was due and assumed it was Demos at last. Calming a justifiably exasperated Yannakis, and trying to assure him that Demos's continued absence was not an insufferable slight to his patiently waiting daughter, had taken yet more precious time.

The next blow had been to discover that the Atrides corporate helicopter stationed at Athens had developed a fault, and the others were scattered at other locations on various company business. Hiring a replacement he proposed to pilot himself—the fewer people who knew about Leandra

Ross's illicit presence on his island the better!—had meant having his own pilot documentation exhaustively vetted by a helicopter company extremely nervous of letting the head of one of the country's largest companies fly and possibly crash himself.

By the time he finally headed east out to sea the bright Mediterranean sun was low in the sky and Theo Atrides was in the worst mood he'd been in for a very, very long time.

Leandra sat on a rock, the sunlight pounding down on her. She stared doggedly out into the blinding sky, constantly scanning the heavens, then dipping back to the horizon again.

Her face was set, skin stretched tight. Her head ached.

In her stomach, fear coiled like a snake.

She had surfaced earlier that day to discover, through her drugged and groggy senses, that she was lying on a bed in a cool, shady room. Although there were few furnishings, it was very luxurious. The large double bed she'd been lying on was covered by an exquisite hand-stitched quilt, and the furniture was dark wood with an antique patina.

Her terror had been absolute. She'd fought for memory.

There was a car. I was pushed inside. Everything went black...

Fear had crammed in her throat. She'd staggered to her feet, lurching towards French windows dimmed with wooden slatted blinds. She had pulled them open. Beyond was a terrace, flooded with sunlight much brighter than it could ever be in England at this time of year. And the scent of flowers was wrong for England—heady and pungent, coming from fragrant blooms tumbling out of ceramic pots. She had lifted her eyes further forward. Beyond the terrace was vegetation—Mediterranean vegetation—and beyond she'd glimpsed bright azure sea.

The house she had emerged from seemed to be built as a long, low series of rooms, one after another, their French windows all closed. Then, suddenly, those of the room at the end of the terrace, where it ended in a vine-shaded patio, had opened, and an elderly woman had come out. She was dressed in black and carrying a bucket and mop.

She'd seen Leandra and nodded her head, smiling. She had set her things down and made some gestures with her hands, clearly ushering Leandra into the room.

Suddenly it had dawned on Leandra where she must be. *Greece! I'm in Greece!*

And if she were in Greece, there could be only one reason why...

Demos. This had something to do with Demos Atrides. It had to—it just had to.

Emotions had coursed through her. One, she knew, was relief. At the back of her mind a dark, hideous fear had been lurking, that she had been abducted and taken away to be white slaved to the Middle East, or worse...

But why had Demos brought her here? And by such extreme means? She wanted answers—fast!

'Demos?' she croaked.

But the woman only smiled and nodded, and made those movements with her hands again. With chilling realisation Leandra understood. The woman was deaf; she was signing.

A bubble of hysteria beaded in Leandra's throat. There was no way she could communicate in sign language with a deaf Greek woman! Then, as a wave of faintness washed over her, the woman was taking her arm and gently guiding her inside the room, sitting her down on a large, soft sofa in front of an empty stone fireplace.

Leandra shut her eyes in confusion and faintness, only to open them again a few minutes later when the woman brought in a tray of food. Hunger clawed in her stomach, and she fell to, swiftly devouring the delicious freshly made bread and soup, washing it down with hot coffee.

A magazine on the lower shelf of the coffee table caught her eye. It was a fashion magazine in Cyrillic. More relief washed through her. She was definitely in Greece and this must definitely have something to do with Demos! But where *was* he?

She combed the villa. It wasn't large, and it didn't take long to realise the only person in it other than herself was the elderly housekeeper. Fighting back fear, Leandra headed off outside. Demos had to be somewhere!

The grounds consisted of an attractively landscaped Mediterranean-style garden, with no lawn but a lot of little stone-paved paths and beautifully tended plants and shrubs. Olive trees were dotted here and there, perhaps remnants of an original olive grove. Instinctively she headed towards the sea, making her way down a little stone path until she emerged some few minutes later on to the edge of a perfect crescent beach.

Leandra stopped dead. It was absolutely exquisite! Gentle waves broke on golden sand. On either side of the beach the land curved protectively, white gleaming limestone brilliant in the sun.

Looking back, she glanced towards the little villa, half hidden by the olive trees.

It was a gem of a place! Very private, very rustic, but with a simplicity that caught at the heart as much as the eye.

But of Demos there was no sign.

Apart from the housekeeper the only other human being was an elderly man watering plants, who must be her husband—and from the way he would only sign to her Leandra realised that he too was deaf.

Her face tightened and she felt fear claw at her again. Instinctively she skirted around the villa, determined to make her way to a public highway and thence to a village or taverna with a phone she could call London from and find out what on earth was going on! At least she had her purse with her, and somewhere she must be able to change money.

She halted dead. She could see no entrance to the villa, no drive leading to a public roadway. Nothing.

The grounds just seemed to stretch on, rising slightly as the contours of the land led gently upwards. She found a pathway and set off. Maybe she could cut across land and find a road further inland. There must be some sort of traffic passing, however remote this villa was. Judging by the absolute silence—not the hint of a sound of traffic, even from far away—it must be pretty remote, Leandra found herself thinking worriedly.

Resolutely she went on, gaining the top of the rise. She paused and looked down. There, below, nestled close to the beach, was the little villa. Beyond it she could see a flat, bare area of ground, the modern metal-framed hangar and windsock declaring it to be a helipad. Just below the helipad was a small cove, with a stone jetty and boathouse, but no sign of a boat. To the front of the villa was the beach, a secret jewel. She swept her eye past the beach, bringing it round to the opposite direction. The sea went with her.

She went on sweeping her head round—and still the sea was visible.

As she completed her three-hundred-and-sixty-degree turn Leandra felt her insides dissolve.

There was sea visible in every direction.

As she stilled, like a statue frozen in disbelief, the truth hit her.

She was on an island.

Theo closed the throttle and cut the rotors. He'd landed. Finally.

As he shut down the controls with routine expertise he glanced out of the helicopter, sliding off his headphones as he did so.

The girl was there waiting for him.

He'd seen her running towards the helipad as he'd made his descent, alerted by the racket the rotors made which was audible all over the island, he knew.

He glowered balefully in her direction. What an infernal mess this was! Cheaper than paying the girl to leave

Demos? Theo snorted. It was going to cost an arm and a leg to sweeten her after her ordeal! And if she chose to press charges...

Sweat pricked beneath the collar of Theo's business suit. He wanted a shower, and a long, cold beer.

He slid the door back and stepped out on to the ground. There was no way he was flying back to Athens tonight. The chopper would need refuelling, for a start, and night was coming on. Besides, he was tired.

Tired physically and mentally.

And his temper was on a knife-edge.

He just hoped the girl wasn't the hysterical type. She must have been frightened by what had happened to her, he found himself thinking as he slid the door to and headed across to her. She was standing very still.

Theo hoped she wasn't going to start weeping and wailing all over him.

He hated that in a woman.

As he drew closer, walking with his customary rapid stride, it dawned on him that if he hadn't known it was Leandra Ross standing there he'd never have recognised her.

The clinging sex kitten was gone. Her lush, slender body, which had been so lavishly on show the other evening, was now almost completely concealed by a sweatshirt and jeans. Her glorious blond hair was pinned haphazardly on her head and her face was completely free of make-up. Yet she was still a stunner.

As he approached he felt his body responding. She had an unconscious grace, standing there, so very motionless—poised almost, he thought, like a nymph of mythical Greece, sighted by Apollo, or Dionysus, or any one of the Olympians in a mood for dalliance, deciding whether to flee from the approaching god or yield to his desire...

Again, just as it had at the gala, the vision that leapt in his mind was vivid. He saw her caught by his restraining arms, drawn close against him, so soft against his hardness, pressing her pliant body against him...

Brusquely he quelled the thought. It was an irrelevance. She was simply a complication—a deadly, dangerous complication now, thanks to Milo!—and she had to be neutralised as soon as possible. That was all.

He stopped in front of her.

CHAPTER THREE

LEANDRA was staring at him as if transfixed.

After hours of staring out to sea, up into the heavens, desperate to spot something, anything, heading towards the island, the approach of a helicopter had sent her hurtling down towards the helipad. Until its noisy rotors had cut through the silence the only sounds she'd heard had been the old man hammering intermittently as he mended an out-house roof and his wife emerging from what must be their living quarters behind the villa to hang up washing.

Then, as Leandra had watched the machine land, a new terror had filled her. The helicopter bore no markings, no Atrides logo.

Oh, God, suppose this isn't anything to do with Demos! Suppose I really have been white-slaved!

She'd felt weak with horror.

Then, as the door of the helicopter had slid back and the occupant had emerged, her eyes had lit on a figure she knew all too well.

Theo Atrides, immaculate in a business suit that must have been handmade for him, his night-dark eyes veiled by a pair of aviator sunglasses, had shut the helicopter door with effortless ease and started to walk towards her.

Something had started to simmer inside her.

He looked so cool, so composed, so immaculate—so imposing. So damn *calm* that Leandra had felt her emotions boil up inside her as if the lid had just been taken off a pressure cooker heated in a furnace.

He'd kept on coming closer. His face set, his eyes hidden by the impenetrable sunglasses that half her mind registered, made him look so ludicrously sexy that she wanted to scream!

And if it hadn't been the sight of Theo Atrides heading towards her as if he could melt butter as he walked that made her want to scream, then something had. Something powerful, and black, and overwhelming, and absolutely, totally raging!

She had been through so much—terrified out of her mind—and now here he was, just sauntering towards her looking like a million dollars.

He stopped in front of her. And the lid flew right off the pressure cooker.

With a frenzied strength she hadn't even known she was capable of Leandra found her hands lifting and starting to pummel, insanely, at the broad chest, thumping and pounding as if she were possessed by all the devils in hell.

Her voice was yelling. She could hear it. Yelling right at Theo Atrides, letting out all the terror and anger and bewilderment and outrage she was feeling—had been feeling all day, since she had surfaced to realise that someone, *someone,* had kidnapped her right off the streets of London, drugged her out cold, and dumped her down a thousand miles away.

And that someone hadn't been kindly, troubled Demos at all! It had been his overbearing, arrogant, *contemptible* cousin, who'd looked at her as if she was dirt. *He* was the one who'd done this to her! And she knew why! To get rid of her! That was why! To make sure Demos couldn't hide behind her, so he could drag him back to marry Sofia!

How dared he? How *dared* he?

Then, abruptly, her hands were seized and held away from him. 'Be silent!'

Her face contorted even more. 'I will not be silent! You kidnapped me and I'll see you in *gaol!*'

'I said, be silent, you virago! Be silent and I will explain!'

Theo looked down at her, his hands like vices around her wrists to immobilise her.

She was a she-devil, a maniac!

Her eyes were flashing like swords trying to pierce him and her chest was heaving raggedly, the breath choking and panting in her throat. Her face was contorted with fury.

And he had thought she might wail and weep!

But at least she had stopped yelling at him. With a hard, heavy command he impelled her to step backwards, increasing the distance between them but still prudently holding on to her wrists all the while.

'Let me go!' she spat at him, writhing against his implacable hold.

'Only if you listen to me!'

Breath shuddering, she gasped, still venomous, 'What's to tell, Mr Atrides? You kidnapped me and I'll see you in *gaol!*'

He swore again. 'I did *not* kidnap you. I am *not* responsible for your presence here, which—' he gave a heavy intake of breath again '—I regret as much as you. Believe me!' he finished crushingly.

He eyed her balefully as she stood there, panting and dishevelled, face twisted like a demon. This was all he needed—a virago flying at him! The perfect end to an intolerable day!

'Now,' he went on, his voice commanding her as if she were the most junior minion in his employ, 'if your hysteria is finally spent, listen to me!'

Heart still pounding in her chest, every limb trembling, jerkily she nodded.

He let her go. Her eyes flashed. 'Well, go on,' she ground out, breath still painful. 'You said you'd explain to me! Go on. I'd love to hear you explain away what you've done to me, Mr Oh-So-Almighty Theo Atrides! And then you can tell it to the police!'

His face darkened at her hostile, vicious tone. No one spoke to him like that! His body stiffened, growing taller and even more imposing, Leandra felt, suddenly shrinking her to about a centimetre high.

'You will not speak to me in that tone,' he informed her coldly, every inch the head of the Atrides Corporation and a man held in respect by all who crossed his path.

It was the wrong attitude to take. The pressure cooker inside her head might have blown its lid, but there was still a whole lot of anger boiling away in the depths!

'Try saying that to the judge sentencing you for criminal abduction and false imprisonment!' she bit back, her chest still heaving with emotion.

He flashed a hand upward imperiously.

'Be silent! I had no part in this debacle, I assure you! And if you will finally condescend to listen to me I will explain what has happened.'

He glanced past her. 'But not here.' He glared balefully down at her. 'It has been a tiring day. I will speak to you in twenty minutes on the terrace. Be there.'

Then he was striding away towards the villa, leaving behind a fuming, shattered Leandra.

Slowly her hands fell to her sides. She could not credit what she had just heard him say.

He dismissed me, she thought incredulously. He kidnapped me, imprisoned me, and now he's just walked away.

Unbelievable, she thought. *Unbelievable!*

Twenty minutes later he walked out on to the patio where Leandra sat at an ironwork table, nerves still shot to pieces. Suddenly she had something else to make her breathing ragged. Her eyes fastened on Theo Atrides and could not move.

Dear God, but he was devastating!

He had obviously had a shower. His dark hair was still damp, gleaming like ebony, and he had changed out of his business suit into casual trousers, immaculately cut, and a polo shirt with a top designer logo discreetly on the pocket. His sunglasses had been discarded and now Leandra could get the full glory of those powerful, hooded eyes surveying her as he approached.

Just as he reached the table and sat down opposite her

the elderly housekeeper emerged from the living room immediately behind the patio, carrying a tray with a glass of beer on it and a pot of filter coffee.

Theo nodded at her, signing a brief response which made her smile and nod before backing away.

'Agathias is deaf,' said Theo, draining a generous portion of his beer as if he needed it, indicating to Leandra that she should help herself to coffee. 'So is her husband Yiorgos.'

'So I discovered,' Leandra said repressively. 'How very convenient to hire gaolers who can't hear their prisoners demanding to be released!'

The night-dark eyes flashed at her.

'As a non-hearing couple, especially of their generation, they find it easier not to be always amongst hearing people. This island they look after for me is a haven for them. But they will return to stay with their family on the mainland when the weather worsens in winter. And they are not, Ms Ross, my hired gaolers!'

'You just admitted this was your island!' Leandra shot back.

'Yes,' said Theo heavily, 'this is my island. But Agathias and Yiorgos are not here to be gaolers, only caretakers. All they know about you is that you were carried in from the helicopter insensible.' His jaw tightened. 'I'm afraid Agathias assumed you were drunk.'

An outraged expression formed on Leandra's face.

'Drunk?' she said furiously. 'I was *drugged*, Mr Atrides! Abducted from Edgware Road and forcibly knocked out! Don't even *think* of making out that I was drunk!'

'Of course I don't think you were drunk! I know perfectly well what happened to you.'

Her eyes widened, her expression instantly accusing.

'My God, so it *was* you who did it! It was you all along!'

A rasp sounded in his throat. 'No! *I* had nothing to do with this, Ms Ross. Absolutely nothing!'

She looked across the table at him, lips thinning.

'Oh? Then who, pray, is responsible? Do tell me!' she enquired venomously.

For a long moment he just looked at her.

'It was my grandfather,' he said quietly.

She started. 'Your *grandfather?* Is he completely mad?'

Theo sighed sharply and reached for his beer again. 'Not mad, no. But old, Ms Ross, nearing the end of his life.'

He looked at her directly. She looked nothing like the way she had at the gala, hanging on to Demos's sleeve!

The memory, which also sent an unwanted kick through his system, reminded him of why he was here. The only reason he was here. To separate her from Demos—and *not* he reprimanded himself grimly, to wonder how it was that her eyes could shift from amber to gold, then back to amber…

'My grandfather is determined not to die before he sees my cousin marry. Demos must surely have told you that he will shortly be marrying a Greek girl?'

He watched her face closely as he spoke. Had Demos told her, or was she wallowing in ignorance of the fact that their affair was going to hit a brick wall any time now?

For her part, Leandra was wondering how best to react. It had just dawned on her that she was going to have to stay in character as Demos's mistress—or completely destroy the whole charade. She thought fast. If she *had* been Demos's mistress, would he have told her about Sofia?

She gave a little shrug. 'I know his *family* want him to marry,' she returned. 'But that's up to Demos, isn't it?'

Her answer was a clear provocation, and Theo took it as such. He ignored her jibe and ploughed on.

'My grandfather is an old, sick man, Ms Ross, who has had much grief in his life. In his…urgency…to hasten the wedding he…' Theo chose his words carefully, as if he were conducting a press interview with news-hungry journalists '…may have overstepped the mark in this instance.'

Leandra felt a spurt of anger. Overstepped the mark?

Abducting and imprisoning her was 'overstepping the mark'?

'He had me kidnapped!' she threw at him fiercely.

Theo's face was unreadable. In his time he'd struck deals worth billions—and he knew how to conceal his feelings when he had to.

'That's a very harsh word, Ms Ross,' he said temporisingly.

'It's a very true one!' she whipped back.

He drank some more of his beer, giving himself time before making his next move. Leandra watched him, eyes narrowed.

'Ms Ross—' Theo moved in again '—I freely admit there has been a gross error committed. You have, most inadvertently, been subjected to an experience which has, I don't doubt, been very distressing...'

Right now, he thought privately, she looked about as distressed as a hangman—eyeing him up as her next customer!

Compunction filled him. She had every right to be angry, he knew. Milo had behaved unforgivably. But he *had* to persuade her not to press charges.

To that end he was prepared to offer her very substantial compensation—providing she also agreed to end her liaison with Demos. Then, at last, he could get Leandra Ross out of his hair and out of his life!

He opened his mouth to start working towards the offer he was prepared to make.

She pre-empted him totally.

'I don't care, Mr Atrides, who gave the orders to bring me here! I just want out. OK? As in out right now. Tonight.' Her demand was crisp, clear, and very insistent.

His expression hardened instantly.

'That's impossible, I'm afraid,' he said immediately.

The amber eyes flashed. He wished she wouldn't do that. It distracted him, and he needed his wits about him now. He didn't need to know how anger made her eyes glitter like gold.

Her riposte came swiftly.

'You flew yourself in, now you can fly me out. Simple.'

'Not simple at all,' he retorted dismissively. 'The helicopter needs refuelling, it's getting too late to fly, I haven't checked out the weather forecast, or logged a return flight with Athens air traffic control, and finally—' he held up a hand decisively '—I am in no mood whatsoever to go anywhere else today!'

Leandra's face whitened and her fingers gripped convulsively at the table surface. 'But I've got to get away from here! I've got to! I absolutely demand that you fly me back to Athens immediately and put me on a plane to London!'

There was a note of panic in her voice, beneath the peremptory order, but Theo ignored it. He was in no mood to do anything other than keep to his firm intention of staying right where he was. He pushed away his empty glass and got to his feet.

'I do not respond to orders—or pleading. No one is going anywhere tonight, and that is final! Now, if you will excuse me, I must contact my office. Please feel free to enjoy the facilities of my island.' An ironic gleam showed in his eyes. 'You may roam at will—be my guest.'

He strolled off, oblivious to the choking sound of Leandra Ross spitting with fury behind him at his parting jibe.

'Agathias will serve dinner in an hour,' he threw over his shoulder. 'Do not be late.'

He disappeared inside the villa and Leandra was left fuming disbelievingly. She was going to be stuck here all night with the insufferable Theo Atrides!

The prospect appalled her.

Changing for dinner did not take Leandra long. After showering in the *en suite* bathroom in her bedroom she could not face putting on the clothes she had worn for nearly two days. But the only other garment she could find was a thin, silky wrap hanging on the back of the bathroom door. Her lips compressed. Presumably it had been left by a former female visitor to the island.

It was pretty obvious to her now just what this island was all about! This must be where Theo Atrides took his high-profile celebrity lovers when they wanted to get away from the flashbulbs of the paparazzi. With only an elderly deaf couple to look after them, they could be as private as they liked.

She tugged the belt of the wrap tight. Well, Theo Atrides's glittering sex-life was nothing to do with her. His only use was to airlift her back to Athens.

Unfortunately, if she didn't want to starve, it looked as if she was going to have to put up with his company for dinner. Defiantly she padded down the corridor on bare feet and into the dining room which opened, she discovered, off the living room.

As she walked in Theo glanced round from opening a bottle of wine.

He stilled totally.

Leandra Ross stood on the far side of the room, wearing nothing but a thigh-length silk wrap belted so tightly at the waist that each breast was moulded in all its glory beneath the taut material. Her long hair streamed over her shoulders, loosed like liquid gold against the scarlet of the skimpy robe. From beneath its short hem her slender legs were like creamy silk. Her feet, arched and narrow, were bare.

Instinctively, just as it had when he had first set eyes on her at the charity gala, Theo felt his body responding to the vision she presented. Desire, hard and insistent, kicked in his guts.

Then another, dampening reaction set in.

Christos, but she was a fast worker!

His mouth twisted cynically. Did she think she could flash her body to get him to fly her back tonight? Was that what this tempting display was all about?

A contemptuous glint showed in his eyes. Or was she after something more than a ride back to Athens? Well, if she thought she could manipulate him the way she ran circles round Demos she was in for a rude surprise. *He* chose the women he bedded—they didn't choose him! And, however tempting a morsel Leandra Ross was, he had no intention—none whatsoever—of making this hellish mess even more complicated than it was already! The only relationship he wanted with her was via his chequebook. Clean and simple.

Even *thinking* of anything else was sheer lunacy!

From her side of the table Leandra saw the expression in his eyes. She bristled instantly.

He's doing it again! Looking at me like I'm trash!

Did he think she was wearing this wrap thing on purpose? Only hunger kept her from bolting back to her room. Defiantly she flashed a scintillating smile at him, as false as it was dazzling, and took her place at the table. What did she care what Theo Atrides thought? He was nothing to her!

There was a caustic look on his hard, handsome face as he sat down opposite her.

If he had been going to comment on her appearance he was prevented by the arrival of Agathias, entering through the door leading to the corridor and the kitchen beyond, carrying a tray bearing bowls of soup which she placed on the burnished table. The smell of food drove away everything else from Leandra's mind and, hardly waiting before Agathias had put a bowl of the creamy liquid before her, she set to.

She ate fast, driven by hunger. Besides, the soup was delicious. So, too, was the delicately flavoured fish which followed. Not bothering to speak to her dining companion, Leandra cleared her plate completely, reaching for a hunk of bread from the basket between her and her host and mopping up the last of the delicious juices. Eating had made her almost forget that she was dining in Theo Atrides's utterly unwelcome company.

Agathias arrived to clear the table, bringing coffee with her. Then she bustled out, leaving them alone once more.

Theo poured out more wine, refilling Leandra's glass. She realised, to her dismay, that she'd drunk rather more than she'd realised. Determinedly she ignored the wine glass and poured herself some coffee.

She felt better now, on a full stomach. The last of the drug seemed to have cleared from her system and her headache was gone. Maybe her mood was better because this time tomorrow she'd be back in London—to sanity.

A shudder went through her. The whole thing had been the most hideous ordeal! Now, calm and well fed, with a large glass of wine inside her, she was filled with incredulity that Demos's grandfather should have committed a criminal act and had her kidnapped.

Even so, her sense of fairness interposed, and she had to concede that no actual harm had come to her. Maybe, she thought unwillingly, she *had* overreacted when Theo had stepped out of that helicopter. She squirmed mentally as she recalled how she had gone berserk at him. After all, she thought grudgingly, he *had* flown straight out to take her back to London, and he did seem pretty appalled by what his grandfather had done.

'Mr Atrides,' she began, her voice slightly husky with nerves, 'I want to apologise for the way I behaved when you arrived. I...I was...very frightened...very confused...I...I didn't know what had happened to me...'

She trailed off. There was a closed look on his face—as though, she thought, he was evaluating what she had said. No, she amended, as if he were evaluating *why* she had just said what she had.

It confused her, making her stare at him wide-eyed, wondering what was going on in his mind.

Then, in a very foreign gesture, he gave a shrug, his broad shoulders moving with perfect musculature beneath the material of his polo shirt, stretched tautly across his chest. The movement distracted her, making her realise just how very perfect that pectoral musculature was. No running to seed for this captain of industry! However he kept fit, he kept very fit indeed...

She snapped her mind back to what he was saying.

'Please, do not apologise. It was perfectly understandable.'

The handsome acceptance of her expression of regret was so astonishing that Leandra simply stared at him. There was something different about him suddenly, she realised, and then worked out what it was. The cynical look in his eye had disappeared. The expression in it now was bland.

'Besides,' he went on, and she heard a new note enter his voice, 'you were, after all, entitled to a display of passion. No woman as beautiful as you should ever have to endure such an ordeal.'

Leandra blinked slightly. What had beauty to do with it? Being kidnapped would be terrifying for anyone!

Theo was talking again. That bland look was still in his eye, and his voice was smooth.

'It is time, I think, Ms Ross, to reach an agreement which will, I trust, conclude this...escapade...on a basis satisfactory to all.'

Escapade? He made it sound like some madcap adventure she'd deliberately got herself involved in!

He paused, curling his fingers around the stem of his wine glass and lifting it to his mouth. She watched, unable to draw her eyes away, as she saw the fingers press with only a fraction of their power around the slender stem, and how, when he drank, the strong column of his throat worked.

He set the glass down. He seemed to have noticed that she had been watching him.

He smiled.

Inside her breast, Leandra felt her heart give a little skip.

She had never seen Theo Atrides smile before. She knew that if she had she would have remembered it in absolute detail. The way his lips indented, showing white, even teeth, and carving deep lines between his nose and mouth.

It was an irresistible smile, one so potent, so devastating, that she could only sit and stare at him.

Suddenly she seemed very short of breath.

And very, very aware that she was sitting here in nothing more than a skimpy robe, an arm's length away from a man who had turned her bones to jelly the first time she'd laid eyes on him—and they were here, on Theo Atrides's very private island, a little piece of paradise where he brought the women he had selected for their beauty and allure to be his personal, intimate companions...

She felt weakness seeping through her, and a creeping, insidious heat.

What would it be like to be one of those women?

What would it be like to be brought here by Theo Atrides and wined and dined, taken out on to that moonlit terrace to feel his arms sliding around your waist, drawn back against the powerful strength of his body, to have those skilled, experienced hands stroke the softness of your flanks, cup the sweetness of your breasts, turn you into his arms and let his mouth plunder the softness of yours, until you were breathless, senseless, boneless...

The vision was so powerful she had to force it away from her. No! Theo Atrides could bring a hundred women here! She would never be one of them!

It didn't matter that he could sit there, looking at her through those dark, heavy-lidded eyes as if he could unveil the contours of her body and make free with them as he would...

She sucked her mind back to reality. And the reality was bleak, and blunt. She had nothing to do with Theo Atrides, nothing at all! He was just the pilot who would fly her back to Athens and put her on a plane to London.

He was talking again, and she forced herself to listen. He was speaking in that same bland, smooth voice, and somewhere deep inside a jiggle of unease began to tingle. She squashed it, and listened to what he was saying. He had leant back in his chair, one hand flat on the table, the other on the arm of his chair. He looked very relaxed.

His deep voice was mellow, and very composed. 'And so, as a gesture of...conciliation...Ms Ross, I am prepared to offer you substantial recompense in consideration of the...distress...you have undergone. I am sure I can count on you to accept it in the spirit with which it is offered, as a confirmation of...good faith...between us. Let us say...' his eyes rested on Leandra, his expression quite unreadable '...fifty thousand pounds.'

Leandra stared. What was he talking about?

'Of course,' he went on, and his voice as smooth as butter, but she could hear an adamantine thread beneath, 'you will appreciate, I am sure, that I must in return ask you to sign certain...assurances...which my legal department will draw up. In addition,' he continued, his voice like cream, 'I am prepared to add as much again as...consolation...for the dissolution of your liaison with my cousin.'

Leandra stared across the table at him. Theo wished she wouldn't. He liked to keep a cool head when he was negotiating, and having those amber eyes upon him was no help. What jewels would he drape her in if she were his? he found himself wondering. Emeralds for her blondness, perhaps? Or sapphires...?

'Say that again.'

There was something strange about her voice, but it was a welcome interruption to his inappropriate reverie. Leandra Ross would get no jewels from him—just hard cash. Fast, simple—and very basic.

'One hundred thousand pounds in all,' he confirmed. There was a note of finality in his voice. He was not about to be bled dry by a woman who had no business making him think of fastening a glittering necklace around the slender column of her throat as his eyes feasted on her lush, luscious curves...

'You're buying me off,' she said slowly.

He veiled his expression at her blunt description, concealing his own revulsion for what he was doing. But he just wanted the whole sordid, ugly mess sorted out.

'Fifty thousand not to complain about being kidnapped, and the same again for dumping Demos. Is that right?'

Her voice was flat.

He inclined his head in silent acquiescence. She looked at him. There was something in her eyes; he couldn't tell what.

'You expect me to accept, don't you?'

He met her gaze. 'It's a very generous offer, and I believe a fair one.' Beneath the smoothness of his voice he was watching her like a hawk. 'After all—' he pushed harder, wanting to put an end to this distasteful process '—my cousin means very little to you.'

Something moved in her eyes then, all right. He felt its sting, and before he could stop himself he heard his voice drawl, openly sarcastic, 'Or are you going to sit there and tell me you're desperately in love with Demos?'

'Of course not!' Leandra retorted.

Scornful triumph flashed in his eyes. Aghast, Leandra realised what she had done—blurted out a truth that would only make him think one thing. And he was obviously thinking it!

'So.' His voice was deadly, and very chill. 'It is, after all, just his money that interests you.'

She tried to recover, floundering to find words that would retrieve the situation, that would wipe that look of condemnation from his eyes.

'You're wrong!' she cried. 'I may not love Demos, but I'm...I'm very fond of him!' The words rushed out of her mouth.

The expression in his eyes changed to one of derision.

'Fond!'

She pushed her chair back and stood up jerkily. She wanted out of here, right now! But first she'd wipe that mocking, derisive look off his face! She folded her arms tight across her chest, quite unaware that it served to raise the hem of her robe dangerously high.

Theo did not miss it, though. His eyes dropped automatically. *Christos,* any higher and he'd be able to put to proof his guess that underneath that skimpy robe she wore nothing at all! He felt his body respond to the thought, and shifted uncomfortably in his seat. Damn the girl! Damn her for standing there and making him want to reach for her, slide her onto his lap and feel her clench his thighs with her long, naked ones...

And damn her for talking about Demos when he wished him to perdition. And the rest of the world too! When all he wanted, with painful aching, was that golden-haired temptress flashing fire at him!

'Yes. Fond. Anything wrong with that, Mr Atrides?'

It was a challenge she should not have issued. Should not have issued at all. Certainly not to him. Not now. Not when she was standing there displaying just about the whole treasure chest of her lush, soft body...

Her arms fell to her sides, loosening the tie at her waist so that the valley between her breasts opened towards the secret jewel of her navel, her hair flowing like gold over her shoulders, her beautiful eyes flashing amber, her soft, lush mouth parted, and her body—oh, that alluring, beguiling body—breasts like ripe peaches, thighs like slender columns leading to pastures of delight...

He felt his own body move. Forwards. Impelled by an urge he could no longer resist. Would no longer resist.

She stood, waiting for him, lips parted. *Christos,* she'd been asking for this all evening, and now she was going to get it!

A lesson he was going to teach her about what was needed between a man and a woman to hold them together...

Fond! She was *fond* of Demos! She stood there, looking like temptation itself, and thought *fondness* was what it was all about—the way to hold a man!

Leandra stared, her limbs as heavy as lead suddenly. She ought to move. Run. Flee like the wind. But she could not. She was as frozen to the spot as Daphne, rooted into laurel, trying to flee from the god Apollo as he came to ravish her.

The breath came hard in her throat. Her stomach was turning to jelly, her limbs to water. But in her veins a flame was running…

CHAPTER FOUR

HE CAME towards her. Stopped in front of her. She could not move. Theo Atrides, potent, overpowering, and she was weak, weak as a kitten, as she stood in front of him. Waiting for him to reach her.

'So...' His voice was a low, deep husk. 'You are fond of my cousin, is that it?' He was looking down at her. His eyes were different. There was not that look of contempt in them any more. Not that blank smoothness. Now there was nothing in them but something even she could not deny, blazing from them like a dark, black beacon.

He was so close to her. Far, far too close... She should step back, away, but she could not. Could not.

He reached towards her.

'But fondness,' he said, and the low, deep voice was a drawl now, slow and compelling, compelling her acquiescence as she stood, staring up at him, so dark and tall in front of her, 'fondness cannot hold a man to a woman. Fondness is far too weak, far too feeble. How can fondness...?' She saw his hand outstretch, felt those long, powerful fingers touch at her throat, sending flickers of debilitating fire through every millimetre where he touched her, stroked her. 'How can fondness match this?'

His fingers glided down the column of her throat, skimming the pulse which had started to beat with low, throbbing insistency. His fingers trailed fire, flickering, licking fire that burnt along her veins, her skin, penetrating deep, deep within her body...

He touched the silk revere of her robe, gliding at its edge along the path of her silky skin, taking the fire with it. Her breath caught, her eyes held by his, dark and lustrous, as his cool, devastating fingers stroked at the faint swell of her breast, easing towards its instantly, insistently aching peak...

He smiled. A devil's smile. Knowing and expectant. Stripping away the lies between them and revealing only the truth—that her body yearned for his like a flower craving the sunlight flooding down upon it...

Her lips parted as she gazed at him, helpless, trapped in that knowing regard, and he smiled down at her, and stroked her tender, sensitive skin, closer, ever closer to its goal, until she thought she must faint with the pleasure of it...

She wanted him to touch her, cup his hand around the straining fullness of her breast, tease the delicate, aching tip to ecstasy...

'You see.' He smiled down at her, eyelids drooping over those knowing eyes that had seen so many women melt before him at his touch. 'You see now, don't you, my tender white dove? *This* is what holds a woman to a man.' His voice was low, speaking to her, only to her...

A primeval moan sounded softly in her throat. She felt her body sway towards him. Faintness drummed at her, and she could not move, not to save her life. Could only feel—feel the endless, endless pleasure of his touch...his soft, arousing touch...

And then it was gone.

Switched off, like a light. His hand was withdrawn and she was left standing there, swaying numbly.

And the smile was gone too. And the dark lustre of his gaze. And the husk in his voice.

He took a step towards the table, reaching out for his wine glass and raising it to his mouth, drinking deeply. As he set it down on the table again he spoke.

It was in a very different voice. Harsh and mocking and sardonic. She was too dazed, too devastated to hear the tight leash of control slammed down upon it by a man who had nearly, so very nearly, lost control altogether. Now he had to claw himself back to sanity by any means he could—whoever paid the price.

'So…' his voice crawled over her '…now we have established that your feelings for my cousin are quite insufficient to prevent you lighting up for any man who strokes that lovely body which you have been displaying to me so generously all evening, let us conclude this matter once and for all.' His voice was harsh now, grating at her like rough wire. 'Take your money—and go. I want you *out*—out of my hair once and for all!'

There was a resolution in his voice that brooked no argument. Had she finally got the message? Theo hoped so—he profoundly hoped so. The effort of walking away from her had been harder than he had anticipated. Much harder.

The harshness in his voice was as much for him as for her.

Folly to have succumbed to the temptation to prove her affections for Demos effortlessly alienable! He had come dangerously, dangerously close to throwing this whole damnable business into oblivion and seizing the one thing he wanted out of the whole godforsaken mess—Leandra Ross, melting that soft luscious body into his…

It had taken all his strength to put her aside. To draw his hand back from where it had ached to go, to curve around the soft heaviness of her breast and graze its thumb over that ripe, succulent nipple he could see thrusting against the raw silk that covered it so sheerly…

But he had done it. There had been no other option—unless it was to sink into a morass so deep only a fool would wade into it willingly.

Leandra Ross was trouble. He had thought so from the moment he had set eyes on her—and her near victory over him now only proved it over again. No woman manipulated him! No woman took him where he did not wish to go.

No more illusions. Never again.

His lip curled. About Leandra Ross he had no illusions. She clung to Demos for his wealth; that was all.

Money would show her true colours.

'Well?' he prompted, wanting this over and done with now, for there was a bad taste in his mouth, getting worse. 'Money is all I am prepared to deal in, Ms Ross. It alone must compensate you for your loss—both of liberty during these last thirty-six hours and of the luxuries you have enjoyed as my cousin's mistress. My offer is one hundred thousand pounds.' His voice was heavy. 'I suggest you accept it gracefully.'

He fell silent, and she went on looking at him.

Her amber eyes were completely empty, drained of all expression.

Then, with a flat voice, she said, 'And I suggest you show me the money first, Mr Atrides.'

'Very well.' His voice was as flat as hers. Something— he didn't know what—seemed to have tightened in his chest as she spoke. Something that closed like an iron grip around him. If he hadn't known better, if he hadn't known all along just what a woman like her wanted most out of life, he might have said it was disappointment.

'If you would wait one moment.' He strode from the room, heading for his office at the end of the corridor.

It did not take him long. When he returned she was still there, standing like a statue. He didn't think she'd moved at all, not a muscle.

Leandra watched him. He had a piece of paper in his hand. The size of a cheque. She held out her arm towards him, turning the palm of her hand upwards.

He placed the cheque in her hand.

She glanced at it, holding it up to check the amount. Yes—one hundred thousand pounds, payable to Leandra Ross. Drawn on the personal account of Th. Atrides, at a very prestigious private London bank.

She looked at it one last time. Then tore it into tiny pieces and let them fall through her fingers on to the floor.

'You—' her eyes had narrowed to fierce, livid slits '—are the most *contemptible* human being I have ever encountered!' Her chest heaved with seething emotion. 'How *dare* you offer me money to buy me off? How *dare* you?'

Her voice rose. 'I can't believe you and Demos have any genes in common whatsoever! How *can* he be related to someone as vile as you?'

She was choking with fury now. Not only had he tried to buy her off, he'd gone and accused her of trying to vamp him!

Her voice was a hiss, venomous with rage.

'And for your information I am wearing this wrap purely and simply because I've got nothing else to wear! Your precious grandfather didn't bother to pack a suitcase for me! So don't flatter yourself I'm wearing it for you! I wouldn't have you if you came stuffed on a plate with an apple in your mouth! You are the most *despicable, loathsome* human being I have ever met!'

She backed away, her face contorted, eyes flashing like laser fire that would shrivel him on the spot. At the door she paused, and spat one last piece of venom.

'Burn in hell, Theo Atrides! Burn in hell!'

Then she was gone, and the door slammed behind her so hard it made the room shake.

Behind her, Theo looked down at the fragments of his cheque, all around him on the floor.

His mouth tightened in black anger.

And total disbelief.

In her room, Leandra sat on her bed, hunched and fearful, hurting and furious. She felt sick. Sick right down to her feet. Sick right to her soul. What a foul, foul man he was! Offering her money. Trying to pay her off. And when he couldn't…when he couldn't…he had resorted to exploiting that dark, brooding sexuality of his, making her melt like putty in his hands…

She blanked her mind, moaning in distress. No, she mustn't, *mustn't* think of that—the way she had just stood there, like a dummy, and let him stroke her—*fondle* her—as if she were a rag doll...

Colour stained her cheeks. She loathed herself. How, *how* was it that her body was so indiscriminate that it could let itself be aroused by a man like Theo Atrides? A man who used his wealth to buy his way out of trouble, thinking nothing of it!

Thinking women were for sale. Thinking *she* was for sale!

Rage replaced shame. That was better! That was much better! Making herself feel her rage and loathing for Theo Atrides was much safer. Feeling anything else about him was far, far too dangerous.

Angrily she made herself see not his dark, tall figure reaching out to touch her, but him standing there with that curl on his lip as he offered her a hundred thousand pounds to buy her off. Yes, *that* was the Theo Atrides she must remember! That and no other.

Keeping that image firmly in mind, she tore off the wretched silk robe, tossing it into a corner, oblivious of the exclusive designer label that made it warrant gentler attention. Hateful rag! To think he'd thought she'd worn it on purpose!

Her teeth ground together, eyes flashing furiously as she yanked back the bedclothes and dived underneath them, squirrelling herself deep underneath the covers as if she would totally shut out everything around her—everything on this benighted island, and especially the serpent that had struck at her tonight.

Sunlight slid delicate fingers of light across the cool, shady terrace running along the front of the villa on Theo Atrides's private hideaway island. It was early morning, and a hint of autumn was finally in the air, even in these warm climes. Dew glistened on the aromatic plants that bordered the paving stones, and brought a diamond beauty to the vine that arched over the patio at the far end.

Theo Atrides stood looking out over his domain. It was

only a fraction of what he owned, but it was very dear to him. He had found it years ago, when his heart was still bleeding—raw from the wound inflicted on it even before the terrible blow of his parents' death, along with his aunt and uncle, that terrible day eight years ago when their plane had plunged like Icarus into the bright Aegean sea.

Now it was the place he came to when he sought solace—but not solitude. In the years since he had been forced to take over the running of the Atrides Corporation he had used it as the one place he could ensure privacy when he conducted the brief, pleasurable affairs which were all he allowed himself these days.

I should come here more often on my own, he thought.

There was a beauty here, a remoteness, a timelessness that brought a peace to him. His mind cast back to all the women he had brought here—so carefully chosen, so eager to please him. So many.

Women from his own world. Rich women, heiresses, wealthy divorcees, film stars and supermodels and opera singers—women he could rely on to be as discreet about their lovemaking as he needed them to be. Women who understood that what he offered was dalliance—sophisticated, pleasurable dalliance. As transient as the waves that broke upon the sand, never reaching into the unplumbed depths of emotion, remaining in the pleasant, pleasurable shallows of his life. Anything more and they would be disappointed.

They had come here, he had enjoyed them, and then they had left. And he had moved on to the next one, and the next.

Their faces merged in his memory; their bodies melded into one another.

A frown creased his brow as he stood looking out towards the sea, so quiet, so still in the early hours of the day. Conjuring up a woman whose face would never blur into another woman's, whose body would never merge into another's.

A woman not from his world at all.

She formed in his vision like a second Aphrodite, rising from the sea, out of its secret depths. Like pale gold she shimmered in his mind, her hair flowing like water, her beauteous limbs gleaming creamily, kissed by the early sun, her breasts like flowers, her sweetness waiting to be plucked.

So much beauty!

Something tightened around his breath.

He tore it free. No, she was not for him! It was impossible!

Pay her and get rid of her!

His face tautened. But she wouldn't take the money he'd offered! Had thrown it back at him as if it were poison! Why? Why had she done that?

Was she trying to get more out of him? Was that it?

Or did she really feel insulted by it?

The thought, once there, could not be thrust aside—no matter how uncomfortable it made him. He didn't *want* Leandra Ross to be capable of feeling insulted at being offered a hundred thousand pounds to relinquish her lover and not see Milo punished for what he had done to her. He didn't *want* her capable of any kind of decency! He wanted her to be venal, and grasping.

Why? Why was it so important to him that she should be someone he could despise?

The answer came crowding instantly.

Contempt for her would keep him safe from his desire for her...

Leandra pulled on her clothes. They were rumpled and grubby but she didn't care. All that mattered was that they were good enough for flying back to Athens in.

With steely determination she kept her mind fixed on the one thing that was keeping her going—the fact that in a few hours she would be back in Athens and on her way home.

She tidied her bed, checked the bathroom was neat and

clean, picked up her shoulder bag and headed out on to the terrace. She would wait there until Theo Atrides appeared, and then she would stick to him like glue until she was safely sitting in his helicopter and lifting off from this benighted, accursed island.

It looked like paradise—but she was mistaken.

The sun was already quite high in the sky. With autumn approaching the days were getting shorter, but the warmth was still a blessing on her face. As she felt the heat of the south on her limbs a sudden brief regret that she would be leaving assailed her. She hardened her heart. It didn't matter how beautiful this island was—she had to leave it. The moment she could.

At the far end of the terrace, where it opened into a patio, she could see that Theo Atrides was already there. Breakfast things had been laid out on the table and he was sitting with his back to her, a phone against his ear. His free hand was gesticulating in short, sharp gestures.

Another minion getting an earful, Lea thought sourly, padding towards him on soft-soled shoes. Well, she didn't care. She wasn't going to speak a word to Mr Theo Atrides, and the only reason she was going near him now was because she was not about to miss out on breakfast.

She reached the table, went to the free side, pulled out a chair and sat herself down, reaching for the coffee pot and a cup in the same movement. She did not deign to look at her host from hell.

Anyway, he was still busy demolishing his hapless minion in terse, brusque tones. She helped herself to bread, butter and honey, doggedly casting her eyes down towards the beach and the sea beyond.

With a final curt command Theo disconnected, and set down the phone.

Hell and damnation! This was all he needed! Yet another crisis to sort out! Out of the blue the head of his US subsidiary was jumping ship. Now he would have to spend the day vetting a replacement and dealing with the inevitable buzz of financial journalists, Wall Street analysts, institutional investors, major customers and suppliers, all wanting to know what he was going to do about it!

He had already just given his media director a grilling over why, pray, it had taken a call at midnight from a prominent business editor in New York asking for his comment to alert him of the impending resignation in the first place!

Face dark, he realised he was staring straight at the figure of his other current first-degree mess. From the way she was ostentatiously ignoring him, she was obviously still fully astride that ridiculous high horse she'd charged off on last night.

Well, this was one mess he was going to clear up right here and now.

'Ms Ross—'

His call for her attention was so expectant of her instant compliance that she found, to her annoyance, that she had turned obediently back to look at him before she'd realised it.

His face was shuttered. Well, that suited her. Leandra schooled hers into similar immobility. She would not lose her temper with him again. She would remain calm and dignified, whatever the provocation. And totally focused on her sole end—getting off this island the minute she could.

And that might be very soon, she registered with relief, as she took in the fact that Theo Atrides was once more arrayed in his hand-tailored power suit, as if he were going to march straight off the tarmac and into a board meeting.

Good! That meant he'd be ready to fly out right away. She couldn't have been better pleased.

He surveyed her a moment, and she held his gaze—blank for blank. Then, abruptly, he spoke.

'You have had the night to reconsider your behaviour. Please understand that I have neither the time nor the inclination to draw this matter out further. I will now write out another cheque for the sum in question. You will oblige me by accepting it without any further hysterics. When we reach Athens my lawyer will present you with papers that he is currently drawing up. You will sign them, and then you will be returned to London where you may cash your cheque.'

He might as well have been speaking to his secretary as to a woman he was trying to extricate from his cousin's bed and prevent from breaking a hideous criminal scandal over his head. Leandra answered him in matching crisp fashion.

'I am not going to accept payment of any kind from you for any reason whatsoever, Mr Atrides,' she informed him in a clipped voice. 'Nothing you can say—or do—will change my mind. However, I am perfectly willing to sign any papers you want that refer to your grandfather instigating my abduction—and I will charge you nothing for signing them!' she put in pointedly.

She looked at him steadily across the table. 'You see, I have, Mr Atrides, absolutely no desire to have my name dragged across the newspapers—as must surely happen if my kidnapping comes to the attention of the police.'

The very thought of what the tabloids would make of a criminal court case involving the kidnapping of a woman painted as the mistress of Demos Atrides, ordered by his own grandfather, aided and abetted by the head of the Atrides Corporation, made her blood run cold.

'However,' she went on, and her voice was chill now, and quite deadly, 'I will brook no attempt by you whatsoever to sever my…relationship…with your cousin. That is no one's business but his own. I appreciate that it is difficult for you,' she finished sarcastically, 'to understand that your vast wealth cannot always buy you what you want, but on this occasion you must remain disappointed.'

Theo looked at her, hearing her out. She was different, quite different from any way he had seen her yet. He had seen her as the clinging sex kitten, the berserk virago, the temptress in *dishabille* last night—and the seething Fury again.

But this Leandra Ross was different again. She was cool, composed, calm and…dignified.

The word sounded strange applied to her. Dignity was not something he associated with women like her. And yet, sitting there, in nothing more than a crumpled sweatshirt, hair loosely tied back at her neck, she had the dignity of an aristocrat, a queen.

Turning his money down.

Money shows their true colours!

In his memory he heard Milo's cynical jibe.

By everything he knew about Leandra Ross, by everything he knew about women like her, she should have been clutching that cheque of his to her as if it were the most precious thing in her life, the very reason for her existence!

But she wasn't. She was turning his money down.

All of it.

Something went through him. Something that scorched through a shell so hard that he no longer noticed it was there.

It made him speak.

'Very well.' He nodded tersely. He didn't want to say more. And he didn't want to think why he didn't want to say more.

She went on looking at him. He reached for the coffee pot and poured out another cup, then glanced at her as he realised she was still looking at him.

'That's *it?*' she said.

He took a mouthful of coffee and set the cup down again.

'There was something else you wanted to say?'

Her mouth tightened. This cool, offhand manner of his was so alien she was confused by it. Then she recovered. If that was the way he wanted it to be, so much the better.

'Only to ask when we are leaving. I am ready to depart as soon as you want. I have no luggage to pack,' she pointed out, resisting the urge to make it sound too sarcastic a reminder of his unutterably false assumption last night about her choice of attire over dinner.

'I will be setting off very shortly,' said Theo Atrides. 'But you will not be accompanying me.'

Cold pooled in Leandra's stomach.

'What do you mean I won't be going with you? Of course I am going with you!'

He shook his head. 'I'm afraid that is no longer possible. Now that you have made it clear you will not accept any money for leaving Demos, I must point out to you that you cannot, at the moment, return to his apartment. My grandfather is staying there while he undergoes medical treatment and examination. You will appreciate, I am sure, that it would be quite impossible for Demos to entertain you as you would wish while he is attending to his grandfather. Accordingly,' he went on, in that same remote, cool voice, 'I must ask you to consent to remaining here a little longer.'

Her eyes stared.

'No *way!*' she bit back.

He raised an interrogative eyebrow. 'Where will you go, Ms Ross, if you arrive back in London with no possibility of resuming your co-habitation with my cousin for the next week or so? Had you accepted my financial aid, I am sure you would have had no problem finding alternative accommodation, however temporary, very swiftly. As it is, where will you go? Do you have resources of your own?'

She opened her mouth to say she had a perfectly good studio flat to go back to. Then abruptly closed it again. Did she want Theo Atrides intruding into her private life? He was bound to want to see her escorted there, whether in person or by one of his minions, and the last thing she wanted, she realised, was for Mr Insufferable Atrides to know anything at all about her real life!

If Milo Atrides was staying with Demos it was obvious she couldn't go back there! As for dossing down with Chris—no, that was too risky as well. Again, she had no wish to draw Theo's attention in that direction!

So what could she do? Where could she go?

As if taking her hesitation for confirmation that she would

be homeless if she arrived back in London, he got to
his feet.

'As I thought. So, you see, it really would be much easier
all round, would it not, for you to remain here a little longer?
As my guest, Ms Ross, nothing more. The island, as you
already know, is very beautiful—' he gestured expansively
with his hand '—and you may regard your stay here as
something of a holiday for you. Everything is at your disposal—why not enjoy a peaceful few days, relaxing in the
sun? Please avail yourself of all the facilities—I am sure
Agathias can find some swimwear for you. And now—' he
glanced at his watch, a gleam of gold at his lean wrist
'—you must excuse me. I can delay no longer. I have pressing matters of business to attend to.'

He strode off, heading down towards the helipad where
the helicopter, already refuelled by him and Yiorgos earlier
that morning, as soon as he had picked up the bad news
from the US, waited for him.

As he went through the pre-flight routines the concentration they required was a balm to him. It stopped him thinking.

Not about who the devil was going to replace his man in
New York, but what he was going to do now about that far
more irritating thorn in his flesh—Leandra Ross.

The combination did not make for a good day. As well
as orchestrating the urgent replacement of his US chief executive, he also had to endure Demos phoning him, urgent
for news. Was his cousin never going to calm down about
his missing mistress? Theo growled silently. Using the US
crisis as an excuse to keep the conversation brief, he simply
told Demos that Leandra Ross had decided to stay on the
island for a few days' rest. He did not elaborate, and certainly did not say that he had tried to buy her off.

And failed.

That was another, very severe source of irritation to him.
If she wouldn't take money, what would it take to sever her
from Demos? He would have to come up with something

fast—an imperative made even more urgent by an invitation he could not refuse: lunch with Sofia's father. It was the last thing Theo wanted to do, but he could not snub Yannakis Allessandros any more than Demos had already done, and to crown it all the man had brought his daughter along as well!

A sweet-natured, pretty girl, Sofia Allessandros sat quietly while her father discussed the business world with Theo.

'She'll make a good wife, *ne?*' The girl's fond father beamed. 'Knows to let men talk business without distracting them. Demos is a lucky lad!'

Theo agreed, as Yannakis clearly wanted, reassured Sofia kindly that Demos would soon be in Athens to claim her, and extricated himself as swiftly as possible.

To his even further irritation, Theo realised that Sofia's docility had not improved his mood. He found himself contrasting it with the flashing-eyed virago he had left behind on his island this morning.

Thinking of Leandra was a mistake. In his mind's eye he kept seeing her, wrapped in that skimpy robe she'd flaunted herself in.

He frowned. Except that she hadn't done it deliberately, apparently. What had she said? Milo hadn't bothered to pack a suitcase for her? His frown deepened. Holding up his hand to silence whatever it was that his group finance director was telling him, he called his PA across to him and voiced his requirement in crisp, low-voiced tones. She departed dutifully on her errand, face expressionless. Then, without missing a beat, he turned his attention back to his FD.

But the damage had been done. Now Leandra Ross had intruded into his consciousness again he could not get rid of her. He needed to see her—or at least let her roam at will through his imagination.

What was she doing? he found himself wondering. Sunbathing on the beach? A vision of her spread-eagled on the sand sprang instantly before him, every limb in perfect display for him. Naked beneath the sun—waiting for him...

He crushed it aside and doused the reaction of his body, shifting uncomfortably in his seat. By the time he had nailed down his new US chief executive he heaved a sigh of relief.

He got to his feet, gathering his papers.

'Gentlemen, forgive me. A pressing engagement. Thank you for your endeavours today on this matter. I believe we can make good progress from now on. I will conference call you tomorrow at ten. Good day.'

He was gone, striding out of the office on long legs.

Heading for a very pressing engagement indeed.

She was there, just as he had imagined. Well, almost. She was not quite naked. A scrap of material still covered that lush, round little *derrière*, but that was a trifling consideration.

She was deeply asleep, he could tell, and the rhythmic rise and fall of her torso showed no signs of disturbance at his soft-footed approach.

For a while he simply stood and looked at her. Pleasure and satisfaction surged through him. Yes, he had made the right decision! This was exactly the thing to do! It solved everything!

His keen brain had applied its usual incisive logic to the situation and come up with the perfect answer to the dilemma facing him. How to detach Leandra Ross from his cousin.

She would not take money—extraordinary as that was for a woman of her kind!—so, Theo reasoned, only one other way was left to him. She had already admitted she was nothing more than 'fond' of Demos. Well—a shaft of satisfaction speared him—let us see just how far 'fond' went!

It wouldn't go the distance, no question!

The way Leandra Ross melted every time he touched her proved that! Theo smiled with feline satisfaction, like a tiger eyeing up a foolish gazelle drinking at a dangerous pool.

He knew exactly what he could do. Would do—very definitely—starting right now. Here on his private beach, below his private villa, on his private island.

He would show Leandra Ross, totally, comprehensively and *consumingly* that she was made for *him,* not Demos! After he had done with her, worked her out of his system, as he had ached to do since he first saw and desired her, she would never go back to Demos! Never!

Leandra was dreaming. Sleep had come to her almost the instant she'd lain down on the soft sand, towel beneath her, the peace and quiet of the island so absolute that her battered spirits had found balm and restoration. Unlike Theo's, her day had been spent quietly—her initial indignation at being stranded here gradually giving way to relaxation, tension gradually draining from her during the long slow hours. As Leandra had lain beneath the warm Aegean sun she had been glad, after all, still to be here on the island. Did it really matter so much to be stranded here a few days longer, in this little piece of paradise? Theo Atrides was gone—and his insulting chequebook with him. There was no reason why she should not take her ease and recuperate from the stress and strain she had endured.

Which was exactly what she had done. After insisting, despite agitated signing to the contrary, on helping Agathias with her housework, she had eaten a light salad lunch on the terrace, which she had prepared with Agathias, and then, choosing the least revealing of the chic, designer labelled bikinis the housekeeper had produced, had headed down to the beach.

A leisurely, steady-paced swim back and forth across the little bay had cooled her nicely, and, pausing only to slather herself with sun-cream she had found in her bathroom cabinet, she had spread out the towel on the sand and herself on top.

And now she was dreaming.

The dream had formed out of the jumbled images tumbling around her exhausted brain. Her dance class, the terror of her abduction, even the noisy thudding of the helicopter seemed so loud it was almost real. And then she was not on board the helicopter but fleeing from it as it chased her across the island, dark and monstrous. Suddenly it had gone, but she still had to run, fleeing from something—something she could not face up to, something she must never succumb to. But she tripped, and fell, sprawling on the sand, winded, and then, as she lay there, the fear of being chased evaporated. It was gone, that threat to her, as if it had never been.

In its place was a voice murmuring softly, like warm honey, filling her with a sweet, soothing languor. It was wonderful! Almost tangible. It was like fingers, soothing down the length of her spine, gently, oh, so gently. She relaxed totally, all fear and tension draining away into the bliss she was feeling.

The lovely, sensuous touch smoothed along the graceful sculpture of her back, drifting like foam from the sea, so lightly she could hardly feel it. And then it was returning, sweeping up to her neck, to that sensitive, oh, so sensitive nape where a million delicate nerve-endings were set flickering.

It was so lovely, so beautiful a sensation, that she gave a soft little sigh, feeling her limbs dissolve into the warm sand.

She sighed again. Those gentling, skilful fingers were smoothing aside her hair, touching at the lobes of her ears, curving down her neck, stroking the hair from her cheek.

In her dream she felt a shadow lowering over her, blocking the warm sun, and as she gave an instinctive, involuntary little shiver it seemed to set all her nerves flickering once more.

Then, soft and soothing, she felt a kiss ease across her shoulder, slow and sensuous...

Her eyes opened.

This was no dream.

The shadow over her was real, all too real. And all too solid.

Theo Atrides lounged beside her, lifting his mouth from her back, his hand from the nape of her neck.

In blind, absolute shock she sat bolt upright, and as she did so she noticed the unfastened bikini top laying crumpled on the towel. She was baring her breasts to Theo Atrides!

CHAPTER FIVE

FOR one long, timeless, unbearable moment Leandra sat there, naked to her waist, while a mere handspan from her Theo Atrides lounged nonchalantly, feasting his eyes upon her uncovered breasts, her golden hair tumbled over her bare shoulders, a second Aphrodite cast up upon the seashore for his pleasure.

A high, strangled sound came from her throat. Then, with a cry of complete horror, she stumbled to her feet, clutching her towel to her. She ran on wings, pelting towards the shelter of the villa, desperate to gain the shelter of her room.

Panting, she fell inside through the French windows. Then, from behind her, her arms were caught, staying her hectic flight. Her sanctuary was destroyed.

'Leandra! It's all right! I didn't mean to scare you!'

He sounded amused as much as concerned.

His hands slid briefly up and down her bare arms.

'Foolish girl,' Theo said, his voice warm with amusement.

It was that that did it. His amusement. He thought it funny, did he? Funny that she'd lost her bikini top and given him a close-up eyeful? With a wild, broken cry Leandra tore away from him, collapsing on the side of the bed in a torrent of tears, hugging the towel to her for dear life.

She could take no more. This was it—this was absolutely it! She'd thought he'd gone, finally cleared off, leaving her alone—and all along—all along he'd just been biding his time. Waiting to come back and…and…*plague* her all over again!

And he'd struck paydirt! He'd finally got his eyeful, all

72

right—seeing her sit there stripped to the waist, totally on show for him!

Her tears ran hotter, burning and scalding, and she clutched the towel, hunched over, sobbing chokingly.

Theo looked down at her. His good mood had gone—evaporated instantly. What was wrong with the wretched girl? What was she throwing hysterics about now? He looked down at her, an expression of sheer exasperation on his face.

He loathed women crying. They only ever did it when they wanted to make him do something he didn't want to. They always wept so—so beautifully! Tears like pearls brimming over, never spoiling their make-up of course, a delicate little sniff of the nose, a few heart-rending sobs, and then some gentle dabbing at the eyes with a lace hanky. A stricken *Oh, Theo, how can you be so cruel to me?* to wring his heart.

And, oh, miraculously, how the tears stopped instantly the moment he gave in to them. Then it would be smiles and cooing again, and *Darling Theo!* until he was sick of that too!

He glared at Leandra. Oh, she was crying, all right! Tears pouring out of her. He frowned. She didn't look the way women usually did when they cried for him. Her eyes were not shimmering like pearls, they were turning red and puffy, and tears were dripping off her chin, which was wobbling ungracefully. And she wasn't giving off any delicate little sobs and sniffs either. Instead, her throat was making great gulps, and she was sniffing heavily in a quite disgusting fashion, trying to wipe her nose on her towel, which she was clinging to as if it were a life raft. And still she was crying and crying like a river in spate.

Theo looked at her. She looked a mess, that was for sure! The frustrated desire he'd been living with all night and all day had withered completely.

He went on watching her a moment. She really did seem to be genuinely upset. He frowned, trying to spot her covertly glancing at him to check his reaction, but she made no such calculating gesture, just descended into sobs that were quieter now, and more desperate-sounding for that very reason.

Not quite realising he was doing it, Theo found himself reaching into his breast pocket and pulling out his handkerchief. It was silk and pristine, monogrammed and gleaming white, quite unused, but he found himself shaking it out with a snap and closing the few paces between himself and the weeping girl.

'Here,' he said irritably, and thrust the handkerchief at her.

She took it with fumbling fingers, not looking at him, and wiped her eyes with a vigorous sweep, then blew her nose, loudly and inelegantly, still gripping on to that ridiculous towel for dear life, as if she were a blushing virgin, not a hot little number who could get him hard in seconds! Then she gave a sniff, rubbed at her tear-stained cheeks with her hands, scrunching up the now-sodden handkerchief.

'I'll wash it out for you,' she said, chin lifting. Her voice sounded thick and choky.

Theo negated her gesture with a dismissive flick of his hand. He looked her over. She looked awful—face all blotchy, skin red and damp, and her eyes were bleary and sore-looking. She looked a million miles away from the pampered little sex kitten who had hung on Demos's arm that night in the hotel's banqueting suite. As for remembering how he had slipped his hand inside that wisp of silk she'd worn last night, or how her sun-kissed body had been splayed out for him on the beach just now—that seemed even further away!

Theo frowned yet again. He was feeling something odd about the girl, but he wasn't sure what it was. It was an emotion he wasn't used to feeling, certainly not about women. Then he realised. He was feeling sorry for her.

He felt himself begin to step towards her, then stopped. He realised what he had been about to do. Smooth the tears from her cheek and draw her into his arms. Not to kiss her. Not to caress her. But to hug her. Tell her it was all right. That he was sorry. That he hadn't meant to make her cry.

Astonishment at his own intention halted him. A sobering thought came to him. He wondered when he had last hugged a woman. For comfort—his or hers. For affection. For kindness.

But why should he feel kindly towards Leandra Ross, who had done nothing but cause trouble and aggravation? It was just that she looked so damn *miserable* standing there, head bowed, face puckered up—no beauty at all...

'Why did you cry?' he asked. His question came out rather more curtly than he had intended. For a moment he thought he saw her flinch back from it. Then she recovered.

'Because I hate you!' she said fiercely. 'You just won't leave me alone!'

There was real vehemence in her voice. For a moment he was taken aback, and then an amused smile slid across his face.

'If you want a man to leave you alone, *pethi mou*, you should not light up when he touches you! Nor,' he added, his amusement deepening, 'should you display yourself to me as naked as a sea nymph, white-breasted like the foam, tipped with deepest coral—'

To his astonishment, at his words a blush started to stain her face. A vivid, violent blush. He stared, completely astounded. For a moment he thought he was mistaken—must be mistaken—for blushing, surely, was something a female like Leandra Ross was far, far beyond. Yet she was blushing all right. And it did as much for her as crying had done. It turned her red as a beetroot and twice as unappealing.

'Why are you blushing?' he asked. There was genuine incomprehension in his voice. 'Because you showed me your breasts?'

He sounded incredulous at the notion.

The blush deepened, running along her arms and suffusing her neck.

'But *why?*'

Leandra screwed her eyes tight shut, then opened them again.

'Because I feel embarrassed!' she let out in a rush, as though he were unutterably stupid to ask.

He stared at her disbelievingly.

'You have no need for any such embarrassment,' he told her. 'You have beautiful breasts, *pethi mou.* Exquisite. High and firm. Full but not heavy. Like mother-of-pearl. They are perfect—quite perfect. You need feel no embarrassment for them! I have seldom seen their like.'

Leandra felt her mouth fall open. He really thought her embarrassment was about having breasts that might not be up to his demanding standard! For the first time in all her sorry encounters with him she was totally speechless. She couldn't even *begin* to find the words to put him right!

As she stood there, gape-mouthed, he went on speaking. His brows had drawn together.

'There is something I wish to say to you,' he announced.

Leandra braced herself. Now what? A flattering reassurance that he found the rest of her body up to his demanding standard as well? A bubble of hysteria formed in her throat. She felt as if she'd just been through a force ten gale—totally battered.

What was he doing here anyway? Why had he come back? Why wasn't he in Athens, or wherever he lived when he wasn't trying to pay people to make them do what he wanted? He'd never warned her he was coming back to the island! If she'd known that she'd have stormed his helicopter this morning and hijacked it back to the mainland! Anything, *anything* rather than have him here again!

Theo steeled himself and spoke. It went against the grain, he admitted to himself, because apologising was something he did only infrequently, seldom having anything to apologise for. But right now he did. So he would do it. He would do it handsomely, and that would be that. It would clear the way ahead and let him get on with what he intended—which was to get Leandra Ross pulsing with pleasure under him as soon as the delicacies of seduction permitted.

'I wish to apologise,' he said, looking across at her. This was not entirely true. He did not wish to apologise, but he realised that he must. Any woman who had turned down a hundred thousand pounds would want to have her gesture appreciated. He was a generous man—he could apologise if it was necessary. And if it meant that at last, *at last,* Leandra Ross would lose the virago act and start to act like a normal woman, eager for his attention instead of fighting it the whole time, then it was an investment that was well worth making.

He frowned as he looked at her. She was still staring at him, lips parted, still clutching that ridiculous towel, his handkerchief screwed up in her hands. Her red colour was fading, and her beauty was beginning to be restored, but she had an expression on her face he could not recognise. He eyed her warily. Was she about to explode again into another bout of inexplicable histrionics? He had never known such an inflammable woman! Not even that opera singer he'd bedded had had such a temper on her! Well, that would soon be long gone. Soon, very soon, Leandra Ross would be purring like a cat beneath his touch.

Right now, though, she was looking at him as if he'd grown an extra head. Now what? he thought irritably.

'Apologise?' she got out. 'You want to apologise?'

His mouth thinned. She made it sound as though he'd just said he wanted to join a monastery or play the trombone.

'Yes,' he said tightly. He could do this. He *would* do this. He took a sharp breath and ploughed on. 'Last night—this morning—you felt yourself insulted when I offered you money. Please understand, I intended no insult. I merely thought that it was an outcome that you would consider…favourable. Clearly I was mistaken. I believe we may now both consider the matter closed.'

There, that should do! He went on, speedily, to the next item on his agenda.

'Now…' his voice changed '…you mentioned this morning that you are suffering from a dire lack of clothes. I have remedied the situation, and once you have…refreshed yourself…with a shower you may select what you wish! I trust you will find something in what I have brought that pleases you.'

He glanced at his watch. 'Perhaps you would like to join me for drinks in, say, an hour? On the terrace? Oh—' he had a sudden recollection as he headed towards the door. 'There should be all the toiletries you require as well. I told my PA your colouring so I hope they will suit.'

He paused again, looking back one last time. She was still standing there, taut as a whip.

'Leandra,' he said softly, 'relax—please. From now on between us there will be only good things. I promise you.' He held her eyes, his own softening. She really was very appealing, standing there with that lost look on her face, wary and confused.

'Trust me,' said Theo Atrides.

Then he was gone.

Trust him. That was what he had said. Leandra veered between bursting into tears all over again or saying an extremely rude word. Trust him? She'd trust a snake more! A serpent!

She shook her head. She was exhausted, she was shocked, she was confused. She didn't know what to do. For a few moments longer she just went on standing there, then with a long sigh realised that the one thing she could do was have a shower.

She padded through into the bathroom.

The shower certainly revived her spirits, and the routine of washing herself and her hair was soothing and calming. As she stepped out and started to dry herself she put her battered mind in gear and started to think.

What was she going to do? Theo Atrides had come back, and it didn't take a genius to work out why. That little scene on the beach had been a dead give-away.

Her expression hardened. Or was there more going on? Was this just the next round in the 'Get Demos Married' campaign? Well, if it was, she had better make one thing absolutely crystal-clear to him. Trying to pay her off with cash hadn't worked—and if he thought she'd meekly tumble into his arms—his bed—and conveniently 'forget' all about Demos then he'd better think again!

She marched out into the bedroom—and stopped short.

Agathias was there, hanging up the last few items of what seemed to be a wardrobe full of clothes. A pile of now empty flat boxes and carrier bags from fashion houses were strewn on the bed. Seeing Leandra, Agathias turned and smiled and beamed, gesturing to the beautiful clothes she was putting away. Then, with a last smile, she pointed towards the enormous vanity case on the chest of drawers, nimbly scooped up Leandra's own clothes, making reassuring washing gestures, and went out. Leandra was too stunned to stop her.

Freshly showered and shaved, wearing comfortable casual clothes, Theo walked out on to the patio with a spring in his step. His mood was excellent. True, Leandra had managed to confuse him again with all that extraordinary crying business, but it was probably just her hormones. Women got overwrought about things—who knew why? And, he conceded generously, she had had a lot to be overwrought about. But all that was over now. As he had told her—from now on there would be only good things between them.

Anyway, her mood would have improved by now, he knew. Agathias would have unpacked her new clothes for her and she would be in seventh heaven! The budget he'd given his PA had been generous indeed—and as for that other item he had brought with him, well, it would take her breath away. He had checked it personally, just now, before placing it in the drawer of the sideboard in the dining room. It was exquisite!

As, of course, was she!

Absently he reached out to check the temperature of the champagne bottle nestling in its ice bucket on the table. Which of the evening outfits would she choose? he wondered. He had asked for several, and, since the exclusive and extremely expensive fashion store he favoured stocked nothing like that tarty little number Demos had been foolish enough to let her wear for the gala, whatever she chose would look breathtaking.

He took a deep breath of the fragrant evening air, anticipating the pleasures of the evening ahead. How quiet it was, how peaceful! Only the cicadas chirruping in the bushes. He looked down towards the sea, dimming now at the end of the day. What more could a man want than a place like this? And a beautiful woman to please him—

Well-being filled him.

A step on the terrace alerted him. He looked round expectantly.

And as his gaze registered the woman approaching him his expression changed.

What on earth was she wearing?

It was definitely not an evening outfit. In fact, he saw as she got closer, it was a beach sarong. The long swathe of jungle-print cotton swept from waist to ankle, but instead of wearing what should undoubtedly have been a matching bikini top she was wearing a long-tailed, long-sleeved, high-necked white and blue striped cotton shirt that should have been paired with cropped pants. It looked totally wrong with a sarong!

He frowned. Did the girl have no fashion sense whatsoever? As his gaze travelled over her he realised she'd done worse than wear a totally wrong top with a totally wrong skirt—she'd hidden her hair underneath a patterned scarf that completely clashed with the sarong's swirling jungle pattern. And she wasn't wearing a scrap of make-up.

Leandra almost laughed out loud at the expression on his face as she approached! Oh, yes, he'd thought she was going to conveniently slip into one of those slinky, sleeveless, low-cut evening numbers he'd so thoughtfully provided! Just right for a spot of fondling later on in the evening! Well, there wasn't going to be any more fondling—let alone anything else!

She reached the table and sat herself down, eyeing the champagne bucket distastefully. Oh, get her liquored up first—was that the plan? Think again, friend!

'I'm afraid, Mr Atrides,' she began, in a prim, tight voice, 'that I don't care for champagne. And I'm also afraid I have bad news for you. I have absolutely no intention of providing your holiday entertainment. I am wearing clothes you bought me solely because I have none of my own to wear this evening, and I am here now solely because I don't intend to starve. I don't enjoy your company, and I wish to endure as little of it as I can! Is that clear to you?'

Her chin had gone up as she'd spoken.

It was a very firm chin, Theo found himself thinking. Firm and resolute. With the slightest hint of a cleft in it that he found extremely kissable. He heard her out.

As she delivered her speech he found he had to control his mouth quirking. *Theos,* but she *was* good entertainment, this Leandra Ross! He found himself highly appreciative. All those endless legions of women who simpered and cooed at him, or threw him sultry come-hither looks, now seemed a total bore!

'Well, I have to say I am relieved to discover that your highly bizarre choice of attire for this evening has a particular purpose,' he murmured, keeping his face straight. 'However, since you tell me champagne is not to your taste, what would you prefer?'

'Mineral water,' she snapped. She could see him trying not to laugh, and it made her cross. He wasn't supposed to be laughing at her.

'Of course,' he said blandly. 'If you will excuse me?'

He disappeared inside the sitting room, and returned a moment later with a chilled bottle of water and a glass.

'I chose sparkling,' he said baitingly, 'to match your eyes.'

Again she could see the humour quirking at his mouth.

She wished it wouldn't. She wished he simply just looked furious, the way he usually did at her. Not just because she was pretty sure he was laughing at her, at her defiance of his evident intention of seducing her, but because when Theo Atrides let humour light his face it made it even more gut-wrenching than it normally was when he was doing his Mr Powerful impersonation.

She shot daggers at him and sat herself down, sipping away at the water he'd poured out for her. For himself, he didn't seem to want anything to drink.

'No champagne for you?' she said sweetly. 'No point in wasting a bottle since I'm not going to oblige you tonight? Still, I'm sure if you phoned the mainland one of your minions would parachute you over a film star, considering I'm off the menu!'

The mobile mouth quirked again as Theo Atrides sat back to enjoy his guest in a way he admitted he had not expected to.

A light gleamed in his eye. 'Are you? But you must remember, sweet Leandra, the night is young,' he said expansively, 'and it is always a woman's prerogative to change her mind! Who knows what the evening will bring? Now, if you wish, let us go through.'

He stood up and gestured indoors. Stiffly she got to her feet and went in. At least he wasn't getting an eyeful tonight, she thought with grim satisfaction. Apart from her face and hands there wasn't an inch of flesh on show! She was covered totally from neck to ankle. She knew she looked daft, that none of the pieces worked together, but their sole purpose was to cover as much flesh as she could—plus her hair.

She took her seat at table. Tonight it was lamb, slow-cooked and meltingly tender, and Leandra ate heartily. Lunch had been a long time ago, and the island air seemed to give her a good appetite. Of the wine that Theo poured for her she drank sparingly, however.

Her host did not, she noticed. Though hardly drinking copiously, he made good inroads on the bottle, clearly savouring what she assumed was an extremely expensive vintage. Yet one more of the many good things in life he indulged himself with!

Well, bully for him!

She found herself watching him as the meal progressed. The fine olive-green crewneck cashmere sweater he wore clung lovingly to his frame, complementing the tanned hue of his complexion. She watched his face, with its strong nose and that wide, mobile mouth. His night-dark eyes, so heavy lidded, met hers from time to time, glinting as they did.

It was as if he could read her rebellious thoughts and found them amusing. It made her stomach tighten even more than watching his face did.

Conversation tonight was more expansive. Certainly it could hardly have been worse than last night. Tonight, Theo seemed to want to draw her out.

'Tell me about yourself, Leandra,' he asked, when Agathias had left the room after serving the main course. 'Are you from London?'

Leandra thought of the bungalow on the south coast she'd been brought up in. She'd inherited it when her parents had been killed, but it was let as holiday accommodation to help supplement her meagre income as a struggling actress.

'Yes,' she lied. She didn't want Theo Atrides knowing anything about her. Anything at all.

'What part?'

'Um—nowhere you'd have heard of.'

'Try me.'

She shrugged. 'Why? What interest can you possibly have?'

'It's called conversation, *pethi mou.* It's what people do when they are having dinner together.'

'I'm not having dinner with you. I just happen to be sitting at the same table as you!'

Theo's mouth quirked again. Taming her would be so very enjoyable. Soon, very soon, the spitting little cat would be purring in his arms.

Smoothly he went on. 'So, you are from London. But, tell me, do you enjoy travelling?'

'Only when I'm not shanghaied,' she returned sweetly.

He ignored her jibe. 'I shall be going to New York next week. Perhaps you would like to come with me?'

She stopped eating, a forkful of food halfway to her mouth.

'New York?' she echoed blankly.

'Yes,' he went on, his voice smooth. 'Come with me.'

His eyes rested on her.

Her mouth tightened. 'No, thank you.'

He smiled, not put out by her reaction. 'Then perhaps Paris would be more to your liking. Or Milan. There,' he said, and his eyes danced, 'you may choose your own clothes, Leandra, since those I have provided so clearly fail to meet with your approval.'

'I doubt it,' she said repressively, refusing to rise to his bait. 'Besides,' she went on, taking the war into his quarter, 'next week I shall be back in London with Demos.'

Right now, even a totally fictitious lover seemed like good protection.

Because, for all her defiance, for all her determination not to succumb to the passing lust of Theo Atrides, Leandra felt weak. He was dangerous to her—very dangerous. And now, tonight, when he seemed to have abandoned hostilities, he was even more dangerous.

Like now, when he smiled.

'Of course,' he agreed, but the glint in his eyes told her he found her reply amusing.

She wished he wouldn't look at her like that. Wished he

would revert back to being insufferable again, so that she could just sit there and loathe him. Of course, she didn't exactly approve of him the way he was now, so calmly assured she was going to fall into his arms like a ripe peach, but all the same the kind of attraction he was generating now was very potent. He was so damn confident of seducing her!

Would it really matter if he did?

The treacherous thought came from nowhere, like a knife to her spirit. Aghast, she crammed it down. Of course she mustn't let Theo Atrides seduce her! What on earth was she thinking of?

She was thinking of how it would be to stop fighting him, to meet his eyes and acknowledge, at last, what had been there from the beginning. To walk towards him and go into his arms, to feel them around her, strong, caressing, to give herself to him and let him do what he wanted with her...

No. No, no and no! She mustn't even *think* like that! It was far, far too dangerous. Theo Atrides was not for her. He never would be. Never.

Shaken by her own inner treachery, she reached blindly for her wine glass, drinking deeply. As she lowered it she met his eyes.

The amusement had gone. In them suddenly, searingly, was only one emotion.

Desire.

For one long, endless moment she just looked at him, her gaze held by his, and between them flowed something so powerful it made her feel faint.

He gave a slow, acknowledging nod.

'Yes,' he said, his voice deep and grave. 'Deny it all you want, Leandra. But it is there. And it will not go away. Whatever you do to fight it—to fight me—if you wore sackcloth and ashes I would still desire you. And I will have you.'

Slowly, very slowly, she shook her head.

'No, Mr Atrides. You will not.'

Humour flashed in his eyes, dissolving their dark, dangerous intensity.

'Well, certainly not if you insist on calling me Mr Atrides! Come, my name is Theo. You must get used to using it! And by the time the dawn breaks...' his voice dropped, husking in his throat, his eyes resting on her with that slow, dark burn in them '...you will be calling it in ecstasy, again and again, until we are both spent...'

The vision leapt in her mind. She saw them, bodies entwined, exhausted in the aftermath of passion, fused together as one being...

He saw it in her face.

'You see?' he said simply, and his voice was low and grave once more.

She stared at him, helpless.

'Why do you fight me, Leandra?' His voice was impelling. 'I am not your enemy. I never was. You have nothing to fear from me, I give you my word. I want only to give you pleasure. What is so wrong with that?'

Wrong...? she thought wildly. There was everything wrong with it! Everything! He was far too dangerous to her! Why couldn't she be immune to him? Why did she have to feel her insides dissolve when he looked at her like that? Why did her heart start to race and make her feel weak in all her limbs?

'Stop fighting me, Leandra, and let me give you the pleasure I know you ache for.' His voice was low and sensual. She felt fire flickering along her veins, stealing her sanity. She tried to fight it, but she couldn't. The noose of his dark eyes had caught her, and she was helpless.

What was the point of trying to fight him—fight herself? Ever since she had laid eyes on him Theo Atrides had set a flame alight within her—one she had never known existed—one she could not douse.

She had tried to douse it—dear God, how she had tried! She had tried to hate him and despise him. She had tried yelling at him and ignoring him. She had wept and she had blushed.

But it had all been for nothing. She knew that now.

The dark allure that was Theo Atrides held her in thrall. Somewhere, somehow, she must find the strength to fight it! To free herself.

But where could such strength come from?

What could save her from him now?

He smiled. A slow, knowing smile. Knowing her weakness to him, her helpless, debilitating weakness that made resistance futile.

'Now,' he said indulgently, 'you have played your little game with me, and it has amused me, but the time for games is over. Go and change, Leandra. Make yourself beautiful for me. Then join me in the sitting room. Agathias will serve coffee and then leave us to be private. Very private.' His voice dropped to a sensual note.

He was so sure, she realised, so absolutely sure that she would simply trot along and do what he wanted, then return and be seduced by him. How very, very convenient for him!

Her mouth tightened. 'No,' she answered, in the prim, controlled voice that at this stage of the game was beginning to irritate him, 'I don't think so. In fact, Mr Atrides—' she deliberately avoided his first name '—I am now going to retire. Goodnight.'

She got to her feet, neatly pushing her chair into the table. She would have liked a cup of coffee, but not if it came with Theo Atrides and being 'very private' with him on a sofa!

She walked towards the door, her canvas soles slapping on the tiles, head held high.

He caught her wrist as she passed.

CHAPTER SIX

LEANDRA tried to jerk it away, but his grip was strong. He turned her to face him as he got to his feet.

'Stop running,' he said softly. 'Stop fighting, stop running, stop…playing…with me.'

There was an intensity in his voice she had not yet heard. She looked up at him. He was so close to her she could inhale the tang of his aftershave, the scent of his raw, potent masculinity. She felt overpowered by him, overwhelmed.

'Let me go!' She pulled at her wrist again and he loosened his grip. His fingers soothed gently at her skin, sending a rich, deep shiver through her. She should pull away—he wasn't restraining her at all—but she could not. She could not.

'Foolish girl,' he said, in that soft, sensual voice, his dark eyes holding her more immobile by far than his fingers around her wrist. There was humour in them, humour and indulgence and desire.

With his free hand he tilted up her chin, cupping it along the line of her jaw, his thumb moving over the lobe of her ear. She felt herself tremble, grow weak.

Her defences fell, without a sound.

'No more games,' he murmured, and drew his thumb along the lush line of her lips, pressing gently until she parted them, with a little breath, a final weakness. He skimmed sensuously along the moist inner surface while her heart started to beat in slow, heavy strokes.

He drew her closer, so that her legs were pinioned between the strong columns of his thighs. She felt herself long to press forward, to feel the whole length of his powerful, hard body against hers.

She gazed up at him, helpless, quite helpless, and felt her captured hand slacken in his grip. He felt it too, and when she let it fall, like the sigh of a feather upon his shoulder, and let her hands curve around the strength beneath, his freed hand found other occupation. It found her hip, smoothing over its gentle curve, sliding behind.

He pulled her in to him.

She gasped, feeling his arousal.

Her reaction pleased him. He moved his thumb along her lip again, sensuously, speaking softly to her.

'You see how much I want you? Go then—go my sweet white dove, before I yield to what I want to do more than anything else and kiss you, and be totally lost... So go swiftly. Make yourself beautiful for me—and when you come back adorn your beauty with this.'

He drew back from her and she felt empty, bereft. What was happening to her? Why was she standing here, swaying as if in a dream, with every nerve on fire with longing—longing to give herself to this man who had such power over her she could not resist, could not...

He reached across to the drawer in the sideboard, sliding it open and taking out the slim, narrow case within. He handed it to her.

'For you, Leandra. For your beauty. For my desire of you.'

She stood a moment, as if dazed.

'Take it,' he said.

She was his, he knew. Relief surged through him. The fighting was over; the games were over. Now there was nothing left but passion and desire. Deep satisfaction filled him. Soon she would be in his arms and he would finally, finally have what he had been craving now for days...

She lifted the lid of the case. A diamond pendant, exquisitely wrought, lay on a velvet bed. It caught the light, flashing with rainbow iridescence. Leandra found herself lifting it out, letting the gold chain slide through her fingers. She looked up at Theo Atrides.

*I could have him tonight! He could be mine! I could lie
in his arms, his bed...*

A wild recklessness filled her. Everything about Theo that
she had spent the last days denying surged through her. She
wanted him badly, hopelessly—helplessly.

She stared across the table at him, lips parted, eyes wide
with longing. He was looking at her. Waiting. His eyes
slumberous with anticipation.

Coldness crept over her. Realisation came hard, riding on
self-disgust. She felt the heavy sharp-edged diamonds pressing into her skin. Theo Atrides was only offering her his
wealth. That was all he was tempting her with. Worthless
money. And that, Leandra realised, with a cold, silent shriv-
elling of all the heat that had inflamed her just now, was all
she was to him. She was nothing to Theo Atrides except a
body to be bought, an object to be enjoyed.

Worth nothing more than diamonds.

Slowly she closed her fist over the pendant, squeezing on
the sharp facets of the jewels as if this pain would obliterate
the pain stinging in her heart.

'Put it on, Leandra, and adorn your beauty for me,'
drawled Theo Atrides, his voice heavy with satisfaction, anticipation.

With a single, fluid movement Leandra hurled the necklace down the length of the table, her face contorted, her
rejection of it—and the man who had given it to her—total.
Then with a broken cry she ran to the sanctuary of her room.

Moonlight pooled on the floor in Leandra's bedroom where
she lay asleep. It was long past midnight. Theo stood, looking down at her.

Her beauty, in repose, was absolute. Her pale hair was
spread like a flag over the pillow, long lashes fringing the
alabaster curve of her sculpted cheek.

As he stood looking down at her an ache filled him.

Why? he thought. Why did he want her so much? Why

was she haunting him like this? Giving him no peace. Other women had never haunted him like this. Why this one?

And why had she run from him that evening, giving that broken cry?

He heard it again, and it caught at him. Piercing him like a needle sliding deep.

Why? Why did she always run from him?

Too many questions. Questions he did not want to ask. Did not want to answer.

He turned away and walked from the room, his face sombre.

It was Leandra who was up first the next morning, dressed defiantly in her crumpled jeans and sweatshirt. She sat at the table on the patio, hands clasped, keeping a vigil. Agathias brought her coffee and breakfast, but Leandra could hardly smile her thanks.

Nor could she eat. A heaviness filled her, crushing her.

She waited.

Time passed slowly.

Eventually, when the sun was already flooding out over the gardens, warming the stones where it reached beneath the dappled shade of the vine, she heard him come. Agathias came with him, setting out fresh coffee and breakfast, and whisking away Leandra's untouched tray with a shaking head.

Theo sat down. After all this time, all this waiting, she could not speak to him.

'Leandra—' His voice broke the silence. It sounded strange.

She looked up, her twisting hands stilling. Her face was bleak.

'Tell me,' said Theo Atrides. The bleakness in her face was like a blow. 'Tell me what I have done. What crime I have committed this time!'

He really didn't seem to know. That was the worst of it— the very worst. Just as he had handed her a cheque for a hundred thousand pounds to buy her silence, to buy her out of his cousin's bed—and thought nothing of it!—now, this time, he really didn't seem to know what his crime was either!

She knew what hers had been all right!

Folly! Unforgivable folly! To let him get so close, to be so *close* to succumbing to him. Well, that was what you got when you indulged in appetites you knew were bad for you, she thought punishingly. And desire for Theo Atrides, weak, helpless, aching desire, was a very bad appetite indeed…

He spoke again. 'Silence won't help, Leandra. If you don't tell me, I can't know!'

Her eyes flashed. No, in his book it wasn't a crime, was it? It was just 'normal practice'! Just like writing out cheques was normal practice! Paying people off.

Buying them for sex.

A cheque, a diamond pendant—what was the difference? Nothing.

'Let's just say,' she replied grittily, 'I appreciate being bought with jewellery as little as I appreciate being paid off with a cheque on your personal account!'

His face darkened.

'I am not trying to buy you! You insult me!'

She stared. 'I insult *you?* Good God, you hand me a diamond pendant and don't think that's an insult?'

'Of course not! Leandra, I gave you that pendant because I know it will look beautiful on you. I gave you those clothes for the same reason. Your beauty cries out for adornment!'

'Yeah?' she jeered. 'Well, pal, *timeo Danaos—et dona ferentis.*'

He stared.

'It means,' she went on in that same gritted voice, '*I fear the Greeks even when they bring gifts.* The Trojan Horse, you know?'

His eyes snapped. 'Of course I know! But how on earth—?' He stopped, looking at her. Then he made a noise in his throat. 'Little cousin Demos, I assume, amusing himself with you.' A hard glint appeared in his eyes. 'And did you object just as much when he gave you those diamond earrings you were flashing that evening?'

She opened her mouth to deny it—then closed it again. She couldn't say that the earrings had simply been hired for the evening—it would expose the charade she'd paraded.

'Ah,' said Theo heavily, leaning back in his chair. 'So my cousin gives you diamonds and you accept prettily. I give you diamonds and you consider yourself insulted!'

She recovered. 'Yes, I do!' Her voice was fierce. 'You insult me all the time! You've insulted me ever since you first laid eyes on me! I can't *believe* you're Demos's cousin!'

'You don't love him. You admitted it.' His voice was scathing.

She glared at him.

'No, I don't. But I'm fond of him. You think that counts for nothing, but it doesn't, Theo Atrides! "Fond" goes a long way.'

'"Fond" is for lap dogs!'

'Don't sneer at him! How dare you? Demos has something you couldn't have in a million years! He's *kind,* and he's considerate. He's a million times nicer than you are!' Her voice had risen. 'So take your jewellery, and your designer clothes, Mr Atrides, and go and give them to someone who wants them, who thinks they're important—more important than kindness or consideration. And don't try and throw sex in my face! I don't care if you're the hottest thing between the sheets since Casanova! I can do without you!'

His eyes narrowed. He did not want to hear her praise Demos to him. He did not want to hear her scorn his gifts and, most of all, he did not want to hear her deny her desire for him!

'I could make you care, *pethi mou.* I could caress your body till you melted from the heat!'

'And then you'd give me another shiny little bauble to

reward me! So much more *tasteful* than handing over money! Men who try and buy sex make me *sick!*'

A rasp of exasperation escaped him.

'Leandra, since gifts from me obviously upset you so much, I give you my word you shall never have the price of a coffee from me! Will that calm you down? You've taken insult where I truly did not mean it. It's my experience that women like being given jewellery. They don't think I'm paying them for sex!'

'That's because they're rich in the first place!'

'Yes, very probably. But the point is I was *not* trying to equate a costly piece of jewellery with spending the night with you! You're a beautiful woman; you know you are! Clothes and jewels adorn beautiful women—that is all. Now—' he raised his hand '—please, let us consider this subject closed.'

His voice changed. 'What would you like to do today?'

'Go home!'

He sighed heavily. 'That isn't possible. You know that.'

'Then you can go home!'

He drew back from reaching for the coffee pot.

'This happens,' he said tersely, 'to be *my* island. Look...' He made a real effort, because everything had collapsed in shards around him and he didn't know what else to do, didn't begin to know how to make Leandra Ross stop fighting him, how to make her yield to him—and the mutual desire that scorched between them.

'Can we not reach some form of...of truce, Leandra? I would like, if it is possible, to spend a quiet, relaxing day. Can you not agree to that without going off the deep end all the time?'

'It's because you keep pushing me into the deep end!'

He sighed again. She was such hard work, this one, but she would be worth it, he knew, finally—finally—when he took her to his bed. 'Right, well, if I try very hard not to do so, will you consent to calm down and accept my peace offering—which involves no gifts, Leandra, no Trojan Horses!—simply a quiet, relaxing day together?'

She eyed him suspiciously. 'I don't want you pouncing either!'

He held up his hands in submission. 'Very well. In exchange for a quiet, relaxing day, I will agree. So, do we have our truce?'

He held out a hand towards her. She looked at it warily.

'Leandra?' he prompted. There was a strange light in his eye.

Slowly, cautiously, as if she was taking a step that might change her whole life for ever, she placed her hand in his.

'A truce,' she said. Then, with a last marshalling of her defiance, she rushed on, 'But don't confuse a truce with surrender!'

He gave a slow, wide smile that reached his eyes, which drooped suddenly, tellingly, at the corners. 'A surrender? Oh, no, *pethi mou*—when you surrender to me you will not, I assure you, confuse it with anything less!'

His eyes dwelt on her face, lambent, expressive, and made her breath catch—before it turned into a choking sound of protest.

'But right now—' he held up a hand to silence her '—I will be content with a truce.'

Leandra twirled in front of the long looking glass set into the armoire in her room. The sun-dress was almost unbearably pretty and beautifully feminine. Despite its designer label it was very simple, in a buttercup-yellow print with tiny white flowers. With its modest halter-neck bodice and gathered waist, floating down to a generous mid-calf length, there was nothing she could possibly object to about it.

Except that Theo Atrides had asked her to wear it.

A truce, she had discovered, meant compromise. And he had asked her nicely—very nicely, in fact, with a wary humour in his face—whether, considering they were going to have a quiet, relaxing day together, she might consent to

choose something from the collection he'd brought for her
to replace her own tired clothes.

Truth to tell, she was glad to get out of her own clothes.
Pausing only to stipulate that she was simply going to bor-
row something to wear, and had no intention of taking a
single garment he'd provided home with her, she had gone
in to leaf through the contents of the wardrobe.

The sun-dress had caught her eye immediately—she
hadn't been able to resist it. Now, as she twirled, her hair
loosened, floating round her shoulders like a golden veil,
she felt her spirits lift. She slipped her feet into a pretty pair
of sandals—when had Theo Atrides paused to check her
shoe size? she wondered—and headed out to the terrace.

The smell of freshly baked bread caught at her. Suddenly
she felt hungry. As she approached the table Theo stood up,
courteously going round to draw her chair back for her, as
if she were a duchess.

'May I tell you that you look enchanting?' he said, and
there was that wary humour in his eye again, as if he really
did think such a compliment might cause her to bristle.

'Maybe,' said Leandra, almost as wary, taking her seat.

He smiled, and their eyes met, fellow conspirators in this
delicate, tentative truce.

She chose a good breakfast—fresh bread and butter, and
sweet Cretan honey—and as they ate she asked him about
the island, and who had lived here before he had bought it.

'No one,' he told her. 'It is too small for a small holding,
but olive trees were planted, and goats grazed here from
time to time. The villa is new, but made from old stone I
had imported from a ruined building I bought elsewhere.
Agathias and Yiorgos' sons work for me, and they were
willing—glad, even, as I mentioned—for the remoteness of
the place.'

She looked around. 'It is very beautiful,' she said.

'Very beautiful,' he agreed, but his eyes were not looking
at his island. Only at her.

She was a chameleon, this girl. She was someone new

again, someone he hadn't seen before. In that dress she looked—she looked enchanting, just as he had told her. Desirable, of course—always that—but the way she sat there, looking as pretty as a picture, he knew he still wanted her, but he also wanted…

He wanted more.

He didn't know what the more was. But whatever it was, he wanted that too.

And Theo Atrides always got what he wanted. He made sure of it.

Leandra's wariness of her host was reaching new heights—and new lows. The reason for the heights was easy to identify. Theo Atrides was exerting himself to be charming to her.

And he was succeeding in spades.

That was the reason for the lows.

She was torn between the two. On the one hand she could obviously appreciate that a man like Theo Atrides, effortlessly running both a vast business empire plus an ever-changing stable of fabulous females, should be well-skilled in the art of making himself agreeable when he chose. On the other hand it was equally obvious he used his charm as a weapon to get his own way—whether in business or in bed.

The trouble was, she realised, that just because she could see what Theo Atrides was doing it did not mean she was immune to the effect. He was pulling out all the stops to charm her. She could see him doing it, know why he was doing it—and still be charmed all the same.

Dimly, she realised that it made him even more dangerous than ever.

This Theo Atrides—the charming, exquisitely mannered, good-humoured, well-behaved version, who sat looking at her, rather than looking her over, as if she were nothing more than an exceptionally pretty girl whom he wanted to admire rather than pounce on—was far, far more dangerous to her than the practised seducer.

Why, she didn't want to think. Wouldn't think.

Would only let herself enjoy, very warily, the day spent in his company.

When they had both finished breakfast Theo left her briefly to call his office, receiving the happy news that all was going well within his empire, including the matter of his new US chief executive. Telling his PA he did not wish to be disturbed except in an emergency, he emerged to find Leandra. He ran her to earth in the kitchen, helping Agathias wash up.

His brows drew together. The chameleon had changed colour yet again! In a hundred years he would not have thought a female like Leandra Ross willing to soil her hands with housework. And she certainly seemed to have won Agathias over—the housekeeper was beaming at her in approval, though she seemed most concerned that Leandra might splash her pretty dress.

He whisked Leandra out to the patio, where Yiorgos had set up a sun-lounger at his bidding in the dappled sunshine beneath the vine. As he settled her upon it he handed her a sheaf of glossy English-language magazines and some popular bestsellers he'd extracted from a cupboard in the sitting room. It wasn't Leandra's usual reading matter, but it was better than nothing and she fell on them hungrily. For himself, he opened his laptop and started to work.

A pleasant hour or so passed, interrupted only by the arrival of mid-morning coffee served by Agathias. Leandra lay, legs extended, warm in the autumnal Aegean sunshine, half shaded by the vine winding overhead, browsing through the magazines while Theo Atrides assiduously worked his way through whatever he was doing, a look of focused concentration on his face. She might not have been present. It suited her, though, for it allowed her ample opportunity to do something she had never yet done to satiation. Feast her eyes on him. Drink him in, soak up the masculine glory that was Theo Atrides.

It came to her, with a shaft of piercing sadness which was really quite illogical, that this time together on his private island was going to be the only time in her life she shared Theo Atrides's company. The sense of sadness—impending loss—intensified. It started to grow into something else, but she did not realise it, caught up in the pleasure of watching him.

Only once did he glance up absently, clearly preoccupied with some business matter, and with a flicker of his dark eyes catch her surveying him. The slightest glint showed in his eyes, the slightest indentation of his mobile mouth smiled at her, and then he focused back on his work again.

All around, the soothing chirrup of cicadas, the rustle of the breeze in the olive trees and oleanders, and the occasional bird song, made the mild warmth very peaceful and relaxed.

Eventually Theo Atrides logged out of his laptop, closed down the lid with a click, tidied up his papers, and looked across at Leandra.

'You're very soothing company,' he informed her. There was a note of surprise in his voice. 'It's a rare trait in a woman.' He looked at her approvingly, and for all her determination not to care tuppence about his opinion of her, she felt herself flushing pleasurably at the mild compliment. He saw her reaction and smiled.

It was a real smile. Not mocking, or amused at her ploys to stop him bedding her, but a real smile. He got to his feet, holding out his hand towards Leandra. The sun had climbed noticeably, and a light little breeze had sprung up.

'Come,' invited Theo, 'we've sat around long enough. Time to take a little walk.' He glanced down at her. 'Hmm, enchanting as your dress is, perhaps it is not quite suitable for an island stroll.'

She went indoors to change, and when she emerged he had too. Gone were the immaculately cut chinos and knitted polo shirt. He had exchanged them for well-worn sawn-off denim shorts, and a white T-shirt which lovingly moulded every muscle in his broad chest and back.

Her breath caught, and she stared openly. Then realised he was doing likewise. She hadn't thought the turquoise shorts particularly tight, or particularly brief, but by the way his eyes were resting on her exposed slender thighs she thought so now. Fortunately, her appliquéd matching top was capaciously cut, with a boat neck and loose elbow-length sleeves.

She dragged her eyes from drinking in his long, muscled legs, fuzzed with dark hair, and his equally exposed biceps and forearms. She would not goggle at him as if he were a pin-up! Nevertheless, she was grateful when, with a decided glint in his eyes, he tossed her a pair of sunglasses—and even more grateful when he veiled his own eyes with another pair.

'Are you wearing sun-block?' he asked. 'You must not burn that lustrous skin of yours, *pethi mou.*'

She nodded in the affirmative. A light tan was one thing—sunburn quite another.

'Let's go, then,' said Theo smoothly, and headed off.

She paused only to knot her hair up into a high swinging ponytail, slide on the sunglasses and hurry after him.

It was a surprisingly pleasant excursion. They talked little, enjoying the silence and the endless views out over the dazzling azure sea. From time to time he took her hand over the rougher terrain, and in his large, warm grip she felt a strange sense of safety. Once he stopped dead, and soundlessly pointed to a lizard, splayed motionless on a rock. It darted away and they went on. Leandra stooped to pluck a twig of thyme, which grew everywhere, rubbing the tiny green leaves between her fingers to release its heady, pungent smell. Theo waited for her companionably.

At the furthest point of the island they paused, looking out to sea.

'Is there anything more beautiful?' he asked.

It was a rhetorical question, and Leandra knew he did not require an answer. This time his eyes really were for the landscape and seascape all around him.

He belongs here, she found herself thinking. He belongs to the sea, and the white brilliance of the land, and the blaze of the sun. This timeless, ancient place whose roots descend for thousands of years. And he is part of it. The thought of it gave her a little tug, somewhere in her insides.

He turned back to her, and his gaze swept past her to encompass all his domain.

'It is a little piece of paradise, *ne?*' he said softly, and then his gaze dropped to her. Again she felt that little tug inside, almost in the region of her heartstrings.

'All you require now is that parachute drop of a couple of film stars!' Her voice was tart, quelling that strange little tug.

A smile quirked at his lip. 'I prefer them one at a time, *pethi mou.*' His brows drew together suddenly, as if something had just struck him. Could that be the reason why she was so reluctant to succumb to him?

'One beautiful woman is enough for me, Leandra,' he said soberly, studying her expression. 'Did you think my appetite ran to more? No, be assured I have no tastes in that direction—or for any other perverse sexual indulgence. One man, one woman—and mutual passion and pleasure between them. That is all that there should ever be. You may rest easy, if that has been worrying you!'

The expression on her face was strange as she heard him speak, and he wondered at it for a moment. Then, as if with effort, she replied lightly, 'Providing they're rich and famous enough, of course!'

His mouth quirked again. 'Ah, so that is your complaint! It is true, I have confined my interests to women who move in my world. But that is for our mutual benefit and protection. This island is as much a haven to them as it is to me, for they live their lives in the glare of gossip and paparazzi.

But that does not mean...' his voice softened teasingly '...I cannot make an exception in your case...'

Something flared in her eyes. 'Oh, slumming, are you, in my company?'

He heard the hurt in her voice and cursed himself.

'No! I did not mean that, Leandra. It was a joke—a clumsy one.'

'Hilarious,' she said, and turned away.

He caught up with her. 'I have offended you—I am sorry.' He took her hand and raised it to his lips. 'Forgive me,' he said.

There was a sincerity in his eyes she'd never seen. It made those strings that were tugging at something very deep inside jerk again. She felt her throat tighten.

She withdrew her hand and he made no attempt to retain it. Well, he wouldn't, would he? She'd got him to promise he wouldn't pounce. It had been rash of her to bait him with those women—even though the answer he'd given had disturbed her. Not about the slumming so much as about his distaste for any kind of sexual perversion...

She had no more time to dwell on this worrying aspect of Theo Atrides, for he was leading the way forward again.

On the way back from their almost completely circular tour, they descended down the low cliff to the jetty on the north side of the island beyond the helipad. There, neatly moored, was a powerful-looking motor boat. It seemed to have appeared by magic, but had presumably been extracted from the boathouse by Yiorgos earlier. A picnic hamper and fishing equipment was on board as well.

'Time to feel the wind in our hair,' Theo remarked, heading for the boat. 'And time to catch our dinner as well.'

He handed Leandra in to the expensive vessel—clearly a millionaire's toy if ever there was one—undid the moorings, jumped lithely aboard and took the helm. Gunning the engine, he carefully nosed the boat away from the jetty, heading for the open sea.

It was fabulous. The Aegean bobbed beneath the gleaming hull as they creamed across the waves. Leandra sat, hanging on to the gunwale, trying not to pay excessive attention to where Theo Atrides stood, legs apart, steering the launch with effortless grace, the wind ruffling his dark hair, buffeting his features. At one point he turned, pointing out the villa as they rounded the south of the island, and grinned.

She felt her heart lift, and grinned back. She knew she shouldn't be having fun with Theo Atrides, but it was too exhilarating to matter any more. He shouted something, but the wind whipped it away. She lifted her face into the onrushing breeze, feeling the spray tingle all over her bare arms and legs. It was wonderful! Glorious!

Theo zipped the launch through the water, evidently relishing its power and manoeuvrability, his masterful control over the sea and the craft. He looked exhilarated as well. He reached the spot he was aiming for, cut engine and dropped anchor. Instantly silence surrounded them. At Theo's direction, while he busied himself setting up his fishing lines, Leandra unpacked the hamper.

It was a simple feast—fresh-baked bread, cheese and cold meats, tomatoes and olives, a bottle of cold white wine, with peaches and pomegranates for dessert.

They ate companionably—Leandra with her bare legs stretched out along the wooden seat in the stern, Theo with his powerful legs splayed where he sat on the starboard bench. Leandra tried hard not to look at the muscled sinews in his thighs, or the way his denim cut-offs strained across his groin. There was a lot of well-developed kit stored away under the tautly moulding material, she reckoned, and then looked away hurriedly, out over the sun-silvered sea. She did not see Theo observe the faint colour staining her cheekbones, or realise that he had witnessed her covert observation of his lounging body.

He felt his body start to stir, roused by her awareness of him, and mused upon whether to dare to sweep away her restrictions—which he would sweep away anyway tonight;

he was determined on it—and take her here, now, on the sea's gently swelling bosom, in the bright clear air, with all her limbs kissed by the mellow sun. The idea was attractive...

One of the fishing lines jerked, and he was diverted.

When they set off back to the island, at a gentler speed this time, Leandra leant back, letting her hair stream in the breeze, her fingers trail in the water. She felt wonderful. Calm and relaxed. As though all the tumult and the tension had been blown out of her, leaving her tranquil and still in the singing silence of the sea.

This is heaven, she thought, closing her eyes and lifting her face into the sun, and quite forgot that she was not here in Greece of her own volition, that she had never asked for the company of Theo Atrides.

As he rounded the headland she watched him steer. He looked so good. She just liked to sit back and watch him. He twisted one hand over the wheel and slewed the boat into a new heading.

'It looks easy!' she exclaimed, before she realised she was voluntarily opening a conversation with him. 'Can I try? I've never driven a boat before!'

Theo glanced over his shoulder and slowed the boat right down.

'Come here,' he said, and she came forward. He positioned her hands on the wheel, letting her feel the pull of the boat on the swing of the sea. Slowly he let the throttle out.

'Steer straight into the sun,' he told her.

He stood behind her, his large frame encircling hers, their legs apart to keep their balance. She could feel his hair-roughened thighs against her, feel her spine pressing back into the breadth of his strong chest, warm and powerful.

Belatedly, she realised this had been a very bad idea.

But it was so exhilarating to drive a boat! As if understanding, he let the throttle out more, his hands over hers on the wheel, and they were warm and powerful too, capturing her fingers with a sweet imprisonment…

The sea and the sun and the salt spray flashed past them. The water thumped against the hull as it parted the sea beneath it. Her hair whipped in her eyes and all she could feel was speed, raw speed! Then, deciding they had left the island far enough behind, he closed the throttle down and came to a halt again.

Hastily she freed herself, and sat down in the gunwale.

'Well?' Theo asked, holding the wheel steady with effortless ease.

'Fantastic!' Leandra grinned. 'Just fantastic! Thank you!'

He cast her a sardonic look. 'So, finally I have found a way to give you pleasure, *pethi mou!*'

Their eyes caught, and held. For a moment complete silence held them as the little boat rocked gently on the swell, caught in a great noose of light from the golden sun.

Something passed between them. She didn't know what. Could not tell. Dared not ask. But it was something so powerful, so strong, so impelling that her breath caught in her throat.

No! Please, no! I can't bear it! Don't let this be happening!

But it was happening. Here, now, under the bright Aegean sky, she was falling in love with Theo Atrides.

And she was utterly helpless to stop it.

CHAPTER SEVEN

IT WAS a sober journey back to the island. The *joie de vivre* had gone out of the day. In its place was a stillness, an expectation. The air was heavy between them, with a strange intimacy, yet not once did Theo touch her, or look at her seductively, or even make her aware of any part of her body.

Yet she was totally, tinglingly aware—and of his as well.

Studiedly she helped him moor the boat and lift off the fishing gear and hamper before they set off back to the villa.

She made sure she walked a little apart from him, not wanting even casual contact with him. That hyper-awareness of him was even more vivid, even more disquieting.

As the villa came in view Theo spoke, breaking the tangible silence between them.

'I must give Agathias our catch. Then, would you like to swim? Shall I meet you on the beach?'

An instant memory of their last encounter there flashed in front of Leandra's eyes. She tried to ignore it.

'Yes—yes, a swim would be great. I'll see you there!'

She almost dashed off, hurrying to get away.

It was typical, she thought in exasperation some few minutes later, as she surveyed the collection of swimwear—it contained no one-piece swimsuits at all, and every bikini was more minuscule than the last. Maybe going swimming with Theo Atrides was a bad idea!

But she couldn't resist a swim for all that. Now that the breeze from the open sea was gone she was heated, and wanted to cool down and refresh herself. The sun was golden and sinking in the sky, and when she padded down to the beach the sand was hot under her feet. There was no sign of Theo yet and, thinking herself lucky for that, she dropped her towel and T-shirt and ran lightly down into the water.

A vigorous, energetic swim back and forwards across the bay did her good. It was only when she was ploughing across for the dozenth time that she felt the water stirring behind her, and in seconds Theo's much larger form was effortlessly overtaking her, with powerful, rhythmic strokes.

Competitive instincts aroused, she increased her own pace, and though he obviously outclassed her she gave him as good a race for his money as she could. At the furthest reach of the bay he hauled himself out on a large flat rock tumbling down from the land.

'Here,' he said, and held down a hand to help her out as well.

She clambered out, winded, and collapsed, gasping. Theo laughed.

'You swim well! But I don't want to tire you out too much, *pethi mou.*' His eyes danced. 'I want you to save some energy for later.'

She threw him a quelling look as she sat herself up, wringing out her hair. It was certainly supposed to be a quelling look, but halfway through, as she met his eyes, it changed. She faltered, the hands squeezing her hair stilling.

'Don't,' she said faintly.

'Don't what?' he echoed. His eyes weren't dancing any more. She wished they were. Dancing seemed safer.

Safer than the way he was looking at her now.

'Don't look at me like that.' Her voice was strained and husky.

Something caught in him. Something about that husked voice of hers, something about the way she was looking at him—something about those slender sun-kissed limbs, that sea-glistening perfect body of hers displayed almost completely, so tantalisingly...

And something more. Something more about her caught in him. It was that strange, elusive *more* again, that he had wanted this morning. He hadn't known what it was, only that he wanted it.

She held the secret to it. He didn't know what it was, but she would show him. He knew that now. Certainty filled him.

Just as he knew that now, tonight—finally—she would come to him.

He laid one long, gentle finger across her mouth.

'Hush,' he said.

And then briefly, swiftly, like the fleetest touch, his lips brushed hers.

A second later he was gone. Plunging into the azure sea, a perfect arrowed dive. Leandra watched him head back to shore, cleaving the water.

He did not look at her as he made his way back across the beach. She could see his body, that powerful, lithe body, gilded by the westering sun. He swept a towel off the sand beside hers, slung it round his neck, and kept on walking.

Alone on her rock, Leandra stared after him until he had disappeared from view inside the villa. Then, slowly, with a strange, helpless feeling, she touched her mouth where he had touched it with his.

That night she wore one of the dresses Theo had had brought for her. It was very simple, very lovely, a column of azure chiffon, like the sea, shot with gold. It fastened at the shoulders with tiny tie straps, then, with a softly folded neckline, drifted down to her ankles. The chiffon hushed around her legs as she walked out to the patio.

There was no sign of Theo. She looked around and then, looking further, saw him on the beach. She walked down to him. He was looking out to sea, into the heart of the setting sun, hands plunged in the pockets of his chinos.

He had spread out a cotton throw across the sand, and nestled an ice-bucket with champagne in it.

Almost she smiled, and then, as Theo turned, the smile died. There was a look in his eye she had never seen before.

It was hunger. Raw, terrible hunger.

For one long, timeless moment their eyes held, exchanging the message that Leandra could no longer deny. Then, with a faint, acknowledging smile, he released her from his gaze and walked up to the throw, to hunker down and open the champagne with a twist of his strong wrist.

The golden liquid frothed into the waiting glasses and he handed her a glass.

Champagne on the beach at sunset—with a handsome millionaire beside me! I ought to think it corny, thought Leandra, sipping the icy golden bubbles.

But it wasn't corny. It was simply—

The word came to her, and she could not unthink it.

Romantic.

But it *isn't* romantic! she thought desperately. Romance is for lovers!

We aren't lovers! We mustn't be lovers!

Why?

The treacherous thought slid into her brain. She groped around, trying to marshal her reasons—her quiverful of reasons—but they evaporated like foam, insubstantial, unimportant.

Instead, she simply gazed at him, eyes huge.

They hardly talked, simply sitting there, letting the mood of the moment ease over them, watching the sun slip into the sea like molten gold pouring over the lip of the world. She sat, legs curled delicately under her like a cat, keeping her distance from him. And he sat, legs bent, slanting outwards, his wrists cupped loosely around his knees, tilting his champagne glass. Behind them in the vegetation the cicadas sounded. A zephyr breeze lifted the ends of her hair, toying with them as if with fingers. She saw his eyes, watching.

And could not meet them.

When the final band of gold had spread out in one last, liquid line along the horizon's edge, and the sun was gone, they watched a moment longer, then, lightly, Theo got to his feet. He held his hand down to help her up. Only for the briefest moment did she let hers slip into his, and let it go again as soon as she had her balance. He scooped up the champagne bottle by the neck, swinging it idly as they walked back to the villa.

The interior was cool, and Leandra gave an involuntary little shiver, pausing to fetch the matching chiffon scarf that still lay on her bed and swathe it around her bare shoulders. When she returned Theo was in the dining room, waiting to take his place. Her champagne glass had been refilled.

Agathias came in, carrying *mezzes,* tasty and appetising, to soak up the champagne, and then Theo fetched the opened red wine, left to *chambrer* on the sideboard, while Agathias served the freshly caught fish, grilled simply with lemon and olive oil and herbs, eaten with delicately flavoured rice.

They talked, but desultorily. It was almost dream-like, Leandra felt. The champagne had lifted her spirits, placing them on a level just out of the stream of things. She felt disassociated, as if reality were somewhere else tonight. She drifted on, as if she were a boat with moorings cut, carried by a slow, inexorable current, heading she knew not where.

Or knew, but would not say.

'Come,' said Theo at the end of the meal, and stood up, holding out his hand to her.

She took it, then let it slip from her. He guided her through to the sitting room, and there a fire had been lit in the huge stone fireplace against the chill of the night. Coffee had been set out on the long, low table before the fire.

I'll drink my coffee, thought Leandra, and then I'll go to bed. Yes, definitely after I've drunk my coffee.

She settled herself down at one end of the sofa while Theo hunkered down to pour out coffee. He was wearing dark trousers tonight, with a black shirt. Leandra had done her best not to look at him over dinner, but now her gaze slid to him, seeing how the material strained across his braced thighs, how the turned-up cuff of the shirt cut the

strong sinews of his forearms, how the open collar revealed
the column of his throat, hinting at the curl of hair still
covered by the shirt...

She took another sip of her wine, which she had brought
through to finish. After the champagne perhaps it was not
wise, but drinking it kept her dreamy state of mind in place,
made her feel as if she were moving through a mist, that
reality was still very away.

Theo placed the coffee in front of her, taking his own,
then sitting on the sofa. Though at the other end from her,
he seemed to dominate the space. Unconsciously she drew
her legs away a little, unwilling to be quite so close.

Leandra looked into the dry, crackling flames in the
hearth. Outside, she heard the sound of Agathias heading
back to her own cottage, her work done. It was only her
and Theo now.

The silence surged around them. Drawing them together.

'So,' said Theo in a low voice, 'you must tell me,
Leandra, what it is to be. This is your moment of choice.
Come to me of your own free will—or tell me otherwise.'

She lifted her eyes across to him.

His voice had sounded solemn. His eyes rested on her.
There was a message in them she could not deny. *Did not
want to deny.*

Not any more.

She wanted to speak, but she could not. There were no
words to say. What was between them was not for words.
Not for reason, or logic, or sense.

For something much more powerful...

He spoke again, his voice low and resonant.

'Silence is consent, my sweet Leandra—'

Her eyes were huge, unbearable, drinking him in, absorb-
ing him into her brain, her heart.

His night-dark eyes consumed her.

'It must be of your own free will. Nothing else. I have
made too many mistakes with you, Leandra. If you come to

me now it must be because it answers the desire between us—the flame between us.'

He leant towards her. She could not move.

He lifted the wine glass from her, placing it on the table without looking at it, without taking his dark, compelling gaze from her.

'If that is not so,' he said, his voice as low, his gaze never leaving her, 'if there is no desire between us, no flame burning, then tell me—tell me now, Leandra.'

He touched her mouth with his fingers, touched along the line of her lips, as gently as gossamer. She could hardly feel his touch—but where she felt it was not in her mouth, but deep, deep inside.

'Tell me to go,' he said. 'Tell me to stop. Tell me not to do this—'

He brushed his finger along her lip, moistening it.

'Or this—' He slipped his hand around her neck.

'Or this—' He drew her towards him, boneless, unresisting.

'Or this—' His mouth covered hers.

His kiss was ecstasy. His mouth moved over hers, easing her lips to yield to him, gently, so gently, she thought she must die of it.

He drew her to her feet, never breaking the kiss, only folding her body against his when they were both standing, the whole sweet, soft length of it, against the strength and power of him.

He held her against the cradle of his hips, feeling himself surge against her.

As if at a signal his kiss deepened, opening her mouth to his like a soft, sweet peach, to taste the succulent fruit within. His hand wound into her hair, holding her mouth to his while he savoured her to the full.

His other hand curved around to span the swell of her bottom, pressing her into him.

He heard her moan, high and helpless, unable to fight him any more, and triumph surged through him.

And relief. Profound, shuddering relief.

She was his!

A growl sounded in his throat and he settled into a slow, pulsing rhythm, laving her mouth, her lips, sucking and grazing, as she gave little moans and lifted her face to his. Her eyes were shut; her long, beautiful eyelashes lay on the pale, opalescent skin. Her hair was falling back off her face, cascading down her spine. Her breasts were swollen against him, and he could feel their hardened tips grazing through the insubstantial gossamer of her dress.

Her hand had wound around his neck, and he could feel her fingers brushing the sensitive skin over the vertebrae at his nape. Her other hand was clutching his waist, holding him against her.

Thunder drummed through Theo as he feasted on her. The moment of possession had come at last! The relief was exquisite. She'd held him off so long, but now, *now* was the hour of satiation. He felt the familiar urgent tension mounting in him, and realised through the dim drowning of his senses that if he did not pull back, and fast, the frustration he'd been suffering since he'd admitted his desire for her in the first moment of seeing her would explode, physically, within him.

And that was not the way he wanted it to be.

He wanted much, much more.

Slowly, with infinite control, he eased away from her, loosening his hold. It was agony. His loins ached as they lost contact with the flesh they sought. He wanted to catch her back, slide the filmy chiffon up her silken legs, lift her up and impale her, sinking himself into her swollen, waiting flesh. Bury himself again and again within her until the stars exploded and the oblivion of bliss embraced him.

But that was yet to come.

He eased her back, catching her shoulders with a swift movement to steady her, for she was swaying on her feet. Swaying with a look of such blank shock on her face that he almost gave a laugh of triumph.

Her eyes fluttered open and met his, pouring down into her.

'Oh, my Leandra,' he breathed, and their breath mingled hotly. 'That, *that* is why you are mine! Your body has known that from the moment I first beheld you, though you have wasted so much time denying it! But now...' He paused, drinking her in. 'Now you will deny me no longer.'

His hands slid down her arms and took hers, holding them gently.

'Come,' said Theo Atrides softly, and led her away.

She followed blindly. In the room behind the coffee grew cold, and the fire in the hearth died slowly down.

Elsewhere, new fires were raging.

He took her to his room, leading her to the side of the bed, his hand holding hers, and she went with him. She could not help herself. She knew with her brain that this was madness. Nothing but madness! Whatever it was that Theo Atrides wanted of her, it was not for all time. Perhaps only for tonight.

But when an eternity without him stretched in front of her, tonight was enough. Tonight was now, and now was all there was. All there ever would be. She would have this of him, then nothing more.

He stood beside the bed and looked at her. She stood in front of him and looked at him. His face was strange. She could see sexual desire imprinted there, blazing with a fierce, dark sensuality that made her bones turn to water. But there was more in his face that she could not read in the dim light.

No matter. For them, the only currency could be desire. Everything else had been burnt away. The rest of the world no longer existed. There was only this moment—now.

'Leandra—' His voice was low, and very husked. He stood tall above her, dark and overpowering. He had overpowered her helpless resistance to him, and now held her with the strongest bonds of all. The bonds of passion and desire.

'Leandra—' His hand reached out and with long fingers stroked down the side of her face, traced along the line of her throat, to pause a moment, his thumb on the beating pulse at its base.

'Your blood beats for me like a wild bird,' he told her, in that low, husked voice.

The fingers traced along the delicate folds of her scarf, dipping across her shoulders, and his wide, mobile mouth smiled.

'This veil inflames me—you inflame me. After all my waiting, now it is time to lift your veil and show me all your beauty.'

He brushed the chiffon from her shoulders and it floated free. His hand slid to her bared shoulder and down the length of her arm, over her warm flank, the soft swell of her hip. As it touched it left a trail of soft fire. His hand slid on, round to her back, gliding up her spine, which arched towards him, to find the concealed zip of her dress.

In one long, smooth movement he had undone it, drawing the delicate material with it. The azure chiffon fell from her.

His breath caught.

She stood in front of him in the dim light as naked as Aphrodite born from the foam. As beautiful. For a moment he did not touch her, only with his eyes. Drinking her in. Desiring her absolutely.

She gloried in it. After all her fears, all her resistance, it had come to this. She stood before him, naked and beautiful. Woman to his man. Desired to his desiring. Knowing that now…now…Theo Atrides, the man she most desired in all the world, was taking her to his bed to make her his. To possess her absolutely.

He touched her slowly.

His hands cupped her shoulders, his fingers resting lightly on the curve of her upper arms, then slowly brushed down the length of them. At her elbows he paused, just holding her there a while as he looked at her—her face, her breasts, which tightened beneath his look alone, even before his thumbs reached out to span the aching peaks which flowered beneath his skilful touch. The pads of his thumbs rested there so gently she could feel no pressure, yet her nipples swelled to him, the tiny indentations on their tips tumescent and as sensitive as swansdown. His fingers slid from her elbows and cupped underneath her full breasts.

He stroked across her nipples, tiny, brief little strokes that turned her spine to liquid and made her sway, weak with desire. She moaned beneath his insistent repeated strokes, as he brushed them rhythmically, arousing them to a hardness she had not known they could possess. Then reluctantly, lingeringly, his hands smoothed downwards, abandoning her breasts which felt cold, bereft, though heat was firing through every vein.

His hands spanned her waist, stroking at her belly button with the edge of his thumbnail before splaying out and down to fasten her by her hips. Again his thumbs moved inwards, touching lightly, so lightly, the tight curls at the juncture of her thighs.

Excitement seared through her. Anticipation. She trembled.

He made a soft noise in his throat, then swiftly, suddenly, he had dropped to one knee. His head bent towards her and she felt, fleetingly, the brush of his mouth on her skin, just above where his thumbs were resting.

It seemed to her to be a kiss of homage—homage to her womanhood.

Then he stood again, swiftly releasing her.

'Lie down for me—lie down for me, my sweet white dove. Let me feast my eyes and then my body—' His voice was low. Impelling.

She lay down on the bed for him, her body limned with light. She lifted an arm above her head whilst the other hand rested laxly, curved at her hip, fingers just edging the curls of her pubis—the unconscious pose of a woman watching her lover—waiting for him. She lay and let him watch her, his dark eyes narrowed, unable to tear themselves away. She felt the power and the glory of her sex, the beauty of her womanhood. Displayed for him—for him alone. No matter if a thousand other women had lain for him, this moment was hers and hers alone. He wanted her and she, oh, how she wanted him. Her nipples tautened again, and the fire laced through her veins.

He stripped his clothes off, steadily, with no visible sign of hurriedness, yet the total unconcern with which he simply let them lie where they fell betrayed his inner urgency. As his naked body revealed itself to her she felt a flush of pleasure wash through her. He was magnificent—a paean to polished muscle, sinew and taut skin. In the dim light that threw into relief the shadows and his strength he was the ultimate male.

As her eyes flickered over his absolute nudity she quailed momentarily. Fleetingly she realised that he assumed she was as richly experienced in the act of consummation as he was. Would he expect an expertise she could not provide? Feel cheated by her exchanging well-practised skill for the only thing she could offer him—absolute desire? The slightest tinge of alarm singed her. Could she even accommodate all that powerful, thrusting masculinity into her unpractised body?

Then all wonderings, all anxieties were over—he moved onto the bed and knelt over her.

A powerful thigh pressed each side of hers. His torso loomed over her. Each hand was lifted and moved, held down by his, either side of her head. She could feel the rearing baton of his sex resting on her belly. Resting before its labours in the long night ahead.

His eyes held hers even as his body held hers.

'Now I have you, my lovely Aphrodite—'

His smile was feral, and a shudder went through her. Of pure sexual excitement. As his dark hooded eyes gleamed down at her something moved within her—powerful, exciting. Dangerous.

'And what will you do with me?' she heard herself whisper, looking up at him, lips parted.

He laughed. Low, triumphant.

'What will I do with you?' he echoed softly, mockingly. Huskily. 'Why, anything I want, my lovely goddess—anything I want...' Slowly his head bent to hers. 'Anything...' he breathed, and his mouth claimed hers.

He kept his word. He was a voracious lover, exacting her absolute surrender to him with the skill of his mouth, his hands, preparing her body for him until she was pleading for his possession, feeding her hunger with his own, bringing her to the brink of ecstasy, unleashing all her restraint, laving her and stroking her until her senses were a single, aching flame of tormenting desire.

He paused just before the moment of absolute consummation. As she lay desperate for his possession, caged beneath his powerful, aroused body, poised to enter her, he looked down at her.

'Is this safe?' he husked.

Safe? This wasn't safe! she thought wildly. This was the most dangerous thing she had ever done in her life! Giving herself to Theo Atrides...

Then radiance illuminated her face. What had safety to do with desire? This rich, wild, sweetness that filled her throbbing flesh? This was beyond sense, beyond reason. This was for wonder, for enchantment—for the emotion that welled like a great tide within her, consuming her.

She would give herself to that. Yes! She would give herself to desire, to wonder and enchantment, to everything that Theo was, to everything he wanted...

'Yes,' she breathed, the word an exhalation. A promise. 'Yes!'

She closed her eyes, lifting her mouth to his. He caught it, possessing its sweetness, possessing her desire. Fulfilling his.

He plunged within her.

She was ready for him, her hips arching in supplication, pleading for the searing invasion of her flesh by his.

For a moment only her body resisted him, then her arousal opened her body to him completely, enclosed around him.

'*Christos*—you're so tight!'

His words were slurred with shock, incomprehension. For a moment, an instant, she felt him hesitate. Withdraw infinitesimally. It was immediate agony. Deprivation. Her clutching fingers pressed into his shoulders. Pulling him back to her.

'I want you!' she breathed, her voice hoarse, gritty. 'I want you, Theo. Oh, God, I want you, I want you!'

Her hips lifted higher, twisting around him. With a low, triumphant laugh he surged again, meeting her twisting hips with a yet more powerful thrust, driving into her. Her senses swam and he thrust again; she cried out, gasping with delight as he filled her completely, her swelling muscles stretching around him, caressing him even as his fullness caressed her. He withdrew a little and she cried out with loss, clutching his shoulders to draw him back. He laughed in triumphant male possession and came down on her again, plunging in to fill her, fuse himself within her, and she cried out again and again as he withdrew and plunged, withdrew and plunged in a pounding rhythm that became the pounding of her blood in her veins. And then, in one final crescendo of sensation, the pulsing spasms of her body convulsed around him. Her throat opened, arching back, and her cry of fulfillment rent the air, mingling with his gasp of triumph as he emptied himself into her. Her straining body collapsed, exhausted beneath him, filled with his seed, fulfilled by his desire for her. By hers for him.

She lay beneath him, panting, dazed. As though she had just taken a journey to an unknown world.

'I never knew... I never knew...'

Her voice was weak, her limbs slack, hands sliding off his shoulders slick with sweat.

'I never knew...' Her exhausted echo trailed away, suffused into a joy so intense it dazzled her.

He lifted himself up on his elbows, only the rapid inflation and deflation of his chest betraying his own exhaustion, his own fulfillment.

'And now you do,' he told her.

His eyes blazed down at her in absolute possession.

CHAPTER EIGHT

BUT not satiation. As she lay beneath him, still so dazed and dazzled that all she could do was stare up at him, bemused, adoring, he dropped soft kisses on her face—her brow, her temples, the corners of her mouth. Kisses that sealed his possession, that marked his territory. She lay passive, sweating, supine. Totally possessed. His hands, loose around her wrists, held either side of her head. Then, as he went on kissing her, murmuring to her in his own language, marking her for his ownership, the kisses started to deepen. At the corner of her mouth he slid across, biting her lower lip softly, but insistently, until she opened her mouth to him again and he drank from that well of nectar.

And as he drank his body quickened within her, and as his tongue moved within her mouth so he moved within her body, hardening himself as he moved, so that she stretched around him, still slick from his seed, and he started to slide, rhythmically, insistently, stroking her, arousing her, himself, building the desire again to red heat, and still more. She moaned beneath his mouth, their tongues twining. Her wrists were held fast now. He was holding her supine beneath him so that he could take and enjoy she who was already his.

This time was slower, with a controlled possession that was a victory lap for his ultimate triumph and pleasure, of which an essential part was bringing her with him. She had to feel exactly what he could do for her, to her, had to moan and writhe and beg for the moment of release that he alone controlled until he judged her ready—not as she thought she was ready, but as he knew she could yet be if she were denied, again and again, past all bearing.

When he let her come she was senseless with desire denied, sobbing at him to give himself to her and so give her her own release. And as he let her go where she ached to go, sobbed to go, he sank inside her, swollen against her flesh, and let her use him for her pleasure as he used her for his, so that she overflowed all around him, through every vein, until her whole body was one engorged, pulsing mass, inflamed and throbbing.

He took her again after that, allowing her no rest, his own body recovering even before hers had ebbed away, so that she was still aroused when he began to caress her again. His caresses turned to sensual teasing and he began to toy with her, stroking the swollen, throbbing entrance to her body with taunting forays of his rigid shaft. She tried to catch at him, clutching his hips, his hard-muscled buttocks, but he laughed again, dark eyes like devils, effortlessly resistant to her urgings to return to her, to sink his tumescent length into her aching flesh and let her feel him hot and thick within her.

'Do you want me, my enticing nymph of the sea?' His question mocked her. She moaned incoherently beneath him, clutching at him again to no avail.

He rolled her over, plunging deep inside her again as he did so, and the rotation and the relief of finding him inside her once again made her incapable for a moment of realising that he had placed himself beneath her. She lifted her head, blind with sensation.

'Lift yourself—come astride me,' he ordered, using the muscled strength of his hands still linked to hers to impel her upright. She sat over him, her thighs slipping down on either side his hips. He moved her slightly, very slightly back, until she was exactly in the position he wanted her to be. Immediately he slid within her, to the very deepest yet, and her lips parted in a gasp. He was pressing to the ultimate, the very neck of her womb.

'Now ride me.' His voice was hoarse. Insistent.

Excitement blazed through her and he could see it in her face. He laughed again.

'You like that, *ne?* Well, so do I, my lovely wanton nymph, with her long golden hair and her naked body, taking her pleasure of me.'

He lifted his head and shoulders with the effortless power of his iron-hard abdominal muscles. His torso was fuzzed with dark hair, the beads of sweat catching the light. Taking each hand in his, he turned them over and softly bit each mound beneath her thumbs.

'Ride me—' he commanded.

She rode him. He held fast her hands, so that she had to grip with her knees for balance, and as she stroked him with her body, rising and falling to impale and re-impale herself on him in wave after wave of mounting pleasure, his eyes glazed with an intensity of pleasure she had not yet beheld in him. It transfixed her, and once in her steady riding she paused in her stroke. Immediately his eyes widened and fixed on her. Again he lifted his head and laved the tender mounds below her thumbs.

'Ride me—'

Dumbly, she obeyed, incapable of resisting a command so absolutely at one with her own desire. Soon her eyes too had the same glazed look about them, and her entire being focused on the intensity of the sensations aroused in her exhausted, over-stimulated body.

She rode him, on and on and on, until her whole body fused into incandescence, igniting over him, around him, and she had to pause in her motion, leaning back as if to rein him in, but only shooting pleasure through herself as his angle of penetration changed and exploded her into a backdraft of searing heat.

She swayed in her saddle as the ecstasy rolled through her and through her, every muscle clenching. His hands gripped hers, keeping her going, keeping her astride, in the saddle of his loins, while her orgasm rolled and roiled, and she pitched and yawed, bucking over him in her extremity.

A long, long time later she stilled, hunched over him, her hands still caught tight, but pressed now between her breasts and the hard wall of his chest. She was still impaled on him, but lassitude overcame her and she began to slip away.

Immediately, insistently, he jerked her back.

'You have had your ride, Leandra,' he told her. 'Now it is my turn.'

He jerked again, bringing her upright again. A grunt of primal satisfaction escaped him as he filled her to her ultimate capacity.

'Ride me—'

Almost she could not obey him—had not the strength left in her body. But his powerful, controlled movements impelled her into her own response.

'Ride me—'

She rode him, rising and falling with a steady, remorseless, pitiless rhythm that took him higher and higher, deeper and deeper. Now freed from the enslavement of her own desires, it was her turn to watch as his eyes glazed to blindness as his whole being focused on this one sensation, this one compelling point of pleasure which mounted and mounted with each impaling stroke until, her hands still held by his, she suddenly saw his face contort and witnessed that almost unbearable moment—his release into ecstasy. He shuddered into her, his expression translated, and watching him come into her suddenly made her weak with awe and mute worship. At that moment he was all-powerful—and all-vulnerable. Utterly dominating her, yet entirely at her mercy.

Wonder flooded through her—wonder and a wild tenderness. As his body jerked beneath her, enslaved by its own desire for hers, she swooped down suddenly, scooping his head between her cradling hands, folding his clenching body to her breasts, holding him close to her, filled with an overpowering devotion to him, an overwhelming desire to hold and guard him from his own vulnerability to her.

She hardly heard her own voice, crooning...

'Theo, Theo, Theo, Theo…'

She hunched over him while he emptied himself into her, utterly spent. Utterly fulfilled.

She folded herself against him, knees gripping his sides, fingers grasping each side of his face, pressed close against him until finally, finally he had stilled, and was hers to hold.

For ever.

Or only for tonight.

It was extraordinary. Leandra's limbs felt as heavy as lead, every muscle exhausted. She could hardly move. Yet she was floating on air. Soaring high into the stratosphere.

It was the Theo effect. The magical, wonderful, incredible, glorious, *radiant* Theo effect!

She stretched languorously, luxuriously. Morning had come after a night of enchantment so strong, so wild that she could not believe it. Yet even though the bright Aegean sun streamed through the window she knew it had been no dream, no fantasy. Last night had been real—searingly, scorchingly real.

Happiness suffused her. She grinned helplessly to herself.

'Theo… Theo… Theo…'

She repeated his name like an incantation.

As if summoned by her calling, the door to the bedroom opened and Theo, a short towelling robe barely covering his powerful body, reversed into the room, carrying a groaning breakfast tray.

Eyes shining, Leandra lifted her arms to him, then let them fall back on the tumbled bed.

'Theo—I've no strength left in me!' she moaned.

He gave a low laugh and set the tray down on the bedside table.

'I will feed you to restore your energies,' he declared. Another promise filled his dark, lustrous eyes. 'You will need them again soon, believe me…'

He sat himself down on the bed, his weight depressing the sturdy mattress. He reached out a long finger and traced the soft outline of her areola as she lay, naked as the goddess of love, in his bed. At his touch her nipple hardened.

He laughed again. A low, husky sound, filled with anticipation.

'Very soon…' he promised.

He fed her morsels of bread dipped in honey, bending to lick away any traces on her lips, deliberately refusing to let her deepen his embrace as she soon, oh, so soon hungered to do.

Once she had broken her fast it was her turn to feed him. He lay back on the pillows like a pasha, powerful, indolent, glorious. She fed him like an adoring odalisque, until he caught her fingers and sucked them into his mouth, then curled his hand around the nape of her neck and drew her down to him.

It took them a long time to surface and pour their coffee.

As he finally levered himself up to perform that office Theo looked down at the woman in his bed.

Her legs were tangled, arms spread out laxly, her hair tumbled across the pillows, her mouth swollen and bee-stung, breasts still half aroused. Her skin had the silken sheen of sweat upon it, still marked in places by the suffused bruising of his lovebites, and the absolute exhaustion of her muscles almost melted her body into the bed.

Theo's heart swelled as he looked at the woman who was his at last. He felt like a king. The emperor of the world! There hadn't been a woman like this for him for a long, long time. In fact, his dazed mind registered, he couldn't think of a woman who had ever had such an effect on him—who left him breathless with desire the moment she had slaked it. A woman he could not get enough of.

A woman who blew his mind away, and a lot else besides. Oh, a lot, lot else besides.

Into his memory a name rang, but he pushed it away roughly. No, this woman—now, here, in his bed—who had fought against his desire for her, his need for her, was nothing like that other one. Nothing at all!

His cousin's dark, accusing eyes swam into his mind's eye. He pushed them away roughly too. Demos had a bride to collect—his bachelor days were over. Leandra had no place in his cousin's life any more. Only mine! thought Theo triumphantly. Mine for as long as I want her—without impediment or obstacle. The future shone brightly with a golden glow.

'I want to remember you like this,' he told Leandra, his eyes lambent, voice purring. 'Imprinted on my memory. Mine, absolutely mine.'

Leandra gloried in Theo's possession. She was his, absolutely, and for this time, while she amused him, he was hers.

She knew, somewhere in the realms of reality, far below the radiant stratosphere she inhabited now with Theo Atrides, that this was only an interlude in time. A brief, precious span of time while he wanted her—before he grew bored and sought new pleasures.

But it was enough.

Later—later would come the pain of losing him. But losing him had been inevitable from that firm moment she had yielded to him. She would endure it, the pain of losing him, but the memory of paradise would last her all her days.

All I have is now. All I have of him is here.

Joy filled her heart as she clung to him, holding him now for all the years to come when he would be lost to her.

After a timeless while, gently but remorselessly, he unpeeled her clinging hands, holding her away from him so that he could nuzzle at her breasts.

'Theo,' she said faintly, 'I can't—no more...'

'I want you again,' he growled. '*Thee mou,* but I want you!'

His skilful lips closed over her nipples, sucking and arousing. She felt her exhausted body respond. Soon he was nuzzling at her with more than his lips, between her thighs. But as he came over her fully, to penetrate her, she suddenly froze.

'Theo—no! I can't!'

His grip on her wrists tightened.

'Do not toy with me, Leandra!'

She heard the frustration in his voice, but her own fear overcame her. She stared up at him fearfully, flinching her body away from where he was trying to impale her yet again with his.

'Theo! I can't! It...it hurts!'

He drew back, frowning. Then, as if seeing for the first time the fear in her eyes, he soothed his hand over her brow.

'Be still—I will not hurt you,' he assured her, withdrawing from between her thighs. He looked down at her musingly. 'You were very tight last night, *pethi mou*. Perhaps that is why you are so...weak now. At first I thought I was imagining things—for there is no reason for you to feel almost as a virgin must! And then I remembered that you dance, and I realised the discipline must have strengthened all your muscles, made you capable of great ...dexterity. It was...' his mouth brushed her temple '...very arousing. Very arousing...'

His mouth worked at her skin, moving down in tiny skimming caresses to her mouth.

'*Very* arousing...' he murmured, and again she felt his body stir against hers, automatically seeking to probe at her.

She tensed once more, fearful of the pain she knew would accompany his penetration. He stilled, and sighed. A fond, regretful sigh.

'Ah, well,' he breathed into her mouth. 'It seems, my lovely nymph, that we must, perforce, move on to more...sophisticated pleasures.' He kissed her once more, then drew back. He rested on his elbow, looking down at her, his finger tracing the outline of her lips. 'Now,' he mused, 'where shall we begin?'

Before the Aegean sun had reached its zenith that day Leandra had become a skilled initiate into just what he had in mind, and whatever last remnants of shyness and reserve had held her back vanished completely.

Theo would permit neither. Nor, as he demonstrated after a long, lazy lunch on the terrace, would he permit any modesty. On the warm sand of the beach, exposed to the sky and the sun, he took her again—so very gently there was not a breath of pain—and then carried her sated body into the shallow water to bathe her in its foaming waves. Then he lay with her, still both naked, under the sun, while she slept in his arms.

When they awoke, as the sun stretched fingers of molten gold over the turquoise sea, he led her back to the villa. They walked through the gardens like the gods of old, in their own private paradise.

Of the serpent there was no sign.

'All right, then, twice in a row! Go on! You said you could!'

'I never promise what I cannot perform—do you not know that yet, *pethi mou?*'

Theo smiled at her, mocking her doubt, and then, with a quick, decisive movement, flicked the pancake high into the air. It landed with a flap, and then soared up again, higher still, so that Leandra gasped.

He caught it expertly in the pan, and grinned at her.

'Three times!' she challenged him, hugging her knees.

They were in the kitchen—she in a pair of casual pastel trousers and a cotton sweater he had bought her, and he, naked to the waist, in denims so tight they outlined every muscle in his buttocks and thighs. And lovingly cradled the bulging pouch of his manhood.

Her breasts prickled. She wore no bra, and the soft, expensive fabric of her sweater revealed the swell of her breasts and the erect buds of her taut nipples.

She ached for his possession again. Their aqueous lovemaking had only whetted her appetite, but he had been cruel. She had begged him to shower with her, but he had denied her.

'No,' he had told her, putting her away from him, where she had clung to his body, pressing her hips into his and circling them enticingly. 'I want you much more desperate for me than this.' He put a finger over her mouth, admonishing her. 'You must learn hunger, Leandra.' His dark eyes roved over her.

She caught his finger in her mouth and sucked on it. He pulled it back, administering the slightest, lightest tap to her cheek. She caught his reproving hand and bit it softly.

'I'm hungry now,' she whispered.

He pulled his hand free and laughed, soft and low.

'Then I will feed you,' he promised her.

But he had brought her to the kitchen, and the commands he'd issued there were focused on sating a quite different hunger.

'Milk, eggs, flour,' he announced, fetching each item and presenting it to her. Then he extracted a food processor, measured the quantities, and told her to switch it on. As the pancake batter frothed he told her to fetch cheese, ham, fruit, cream, syrup, chocolate.

'Food for the gods.' He laughed. 'Simple, quick, nutritious and very versatile. Stand back! This pan is hot!'

It *was* a feast fit for the gods, full of laughter and appetite, as they sat across from each other at the scrubbed table, demolishing their stack of pancakes, helping themselves to the array of savoury and sweet accompaniments.

She had never in all her life enjoyed a meal more.

They washed it down with vintage champagne.

Then they went back to bed, and Leandra discovered exactly, *exactly,* what hunger could do when it was unleashed on a naked, aroused body.

Their coupling was like a burning forest fire, consuming them. All night, again and again, satiation yielded to renewed desire until once more her body was a mindless pulp of inflamed arousal. Again and again he took her to the brink, and plunged over with her, so that their cries mingled in the dark night air, echoing to the starry heavens.

Once he led her outside, and in the chill air leant her back against the still sun-warmed whitewashed wall of the house and took her beneath the stars themselves, lifting her body up on his like a homage to the heavens. Then, released again, her ecstasy burnt out, she ran with bare feet, bare body, like an elven creature of the night, down to the beach.

'Catch me!' she cried, her hair streaming in the starlight.

He sprinted after her, allowing her the pleasure of evading him until he chose to close the distance and bring her down with a tackle that drove the breath from her body. They collapsed upon the sand, rolling over and over, breathless with laughter, until he clasped her to him and scooped her up, ran with her to the tumbling waves and tossed her laughing in.

Her shriek was drowned in water, and he dived after her. She shrieked again and lurched away from him, diving down and under, and up and through the waves and the inky water, until he caught her by her wet streaming hair and kissed her, and picked her up and carried her out of the sea like Aphrodite herself, and back to his bed for his possession.

She was an inhabitant of paradise.

But in the morning the serpent returned, destroying all her bliss.

* * *

She had no warning of it.

They had just made love. Leandra was lying in the fold of his arm, wrapped around her shoulder, spent and languorous, her cheek against his hair-roughened chest as he held her loosely to his side.

'Tell me,' he said, his voice low and sonorous, 'have you been to New York?'

'No.' She smiled, letting her hand play idly over the taut muscles of his abdomen.

'Good.' He sounded satisfied. 'Then I shall have the pleasure of showing it off to you—and you to it! I told you I would need to go there next week.' A frown creased his brow momentarily. 'Do you have a passport?'

'Uh-huh,' she murmured drowsily.

New York! The words glowed before her eyes. He could have told her he was taking her to Death Valley and her bliss would have been the same.

He wants me to go with him!

Happiness and relief seared through her. However brief, however transient this time was with Theo, to know that it would not end here, on this island paradise, was a wonder and a joy to her!

As she rejoiced that he had not yet grown weary of her she felt his hand brush at her arm. He was speaking again.

'I will have your passport brought to Athens. The agency my grandfather used to bring you here managed to evade the immigration formalities, but you will need it if we are to travel.' A frown creased his brow. Her passport must be in Demos's apartment, and the reminder that she had once been part of his cousin's life was unwelcome. Then his brow cleared. That was gone now—all gone. Leandra was his— and would remain so for as long as he wanted her.

And *how* he still wanted her! His appetite for her was insatiable! She was as fresh and sweet for him now as she had been the first time he had taken her!

And more so! There was something about her—something about Leandra Ross—that captivated him! He still didn't know what that elusive 'more' was that had so drawn him to her, but he would find out. Oh, he would find out!

However long it took, he would find out what it was that he wanted from Leandra Ross—more than the absolute sensual consummation that he already possessed, supreme though that was.

He would keep her until he had it. However long it took.

The thought bathed a radiant, glorious light over him.

Another thought struck him, banal in the extreme, but while he was in practical mode, he might as well deal with it—and then... He could feel his body hardening already, recovering from its total exhaustion of a few minutes ago. Then he would put aside all banalities and sink once more into the bottomless well of desire...

'Is there anything else you need from London, Leandra?' he asked. 'Personal effects—that sort of thing. I don't mean clothes—I will buy you everything you need! Oh, and you had better tell me if you have sufficient supply of the Pill. I can have your doctor contacted for a repeat prescription if you need more—or you can see a doctor in Athens if you prefer.'

He smiled down at her, his heavy-lidded eyes dark and lustrous. She looked up into his eyes, feeling her breath catch. Bliss filled her.

'Well?' he prompted absently, busying himself with brushing her arm idly.

'What?' she murmured, distracted by the delicious sensation he was arousing.

'The Pill—do you need any more or have you got enough?'

Her skin was tingling with soft pleasure where his fingers lightly touched.

'I'm not on the Pill,' she replied. She pressed her mouth

against his chest, shifting her weight a little on her hips so she could turn her body into his more closely.

A hand gripped her elbow. The stroking had stopped.

'Then what are you using for contraception?'

CHAPTER NINE

HIS voice was different. She lifted her mouth away and tilted her head towards him.

He was looking at her, head lifted off the pillow. There was no indulgence in his face, only a demand to be answered.

'You told me it was safe.'

She stared at him. What did he mean? He sat up, pulling away from her.

'Before I made love to you. You told me it was safe.'

His voice was still different. Fear licked at her. What was happening? Why was he being like this? What had she done?

Contraception. He was talking about contraception. She had not thought about it. Had blanked it out. She had realised belatedly, some time in the long hours of that first night together, that Theo had used no protection himself. She knew she should care, but she did not. Could not. She gloried in the freedom it gave their lovemaking—and she was safe enough. Her period was due any day now—surely she was safe?

Abruptly he got out of bed. Pulling on his towelling dressing robe, he knotted the belt tightly. When he looked at Leandra again his face, she realised, had simply closed.

'Theo—' Her voice sounded strained, fighting down panic. What was happening?

He did not answer.

'I have been away from my office too long,' he announced. 'Forgive me, but I will have to leave you alone today.'

She studied his face anxiously. Something had happened. She knew it had.

And she knew what it was. As she watched him stride off into the bathroom and shut the door behind him her stomach started to churn.

He was worried because she had used no contraception.

Well, of course he's worried! What do you imagine? And you should be worried too!

Dismay flooded her, and shame. How could she have been so stupid as not to think about the consequences of what she had done? She had done the one thing that no woman anywhere ever did—she had had unprotected sex with a man, carried away by her own selfish self-indulgence! She had behaved like the most irresponsible teenager in the world! Shutting out anything that might interfere with the reckless abandon that had consumed her. Thoughtless, selfish, feckless...

I could be pregnant!

She waited for the horror to strike her as she made the admission to herself—but instead of horror a huge, ballooning wave of delight filled her. Pregnant—pregnant with Theo's child!

For an instant, as brief as it was blissful, she felt filled with such happiness she could not believe it. She could be carrying Theo's child!

The balloon burst. Fool—you fool! How irresponsible can you be? Wanting to bear a child for a man to whom you are nothing more than a seductive interlude! Oh, don't give yourself grand ideas, my girl—he's all over you now, but you knew—you *knew* it meant nothing to him...you *knew*...

And his reaction just now is all the proof of that you need. Did you see bliss on his face when you blurted out you weren't on the Pill? Did you? You think a man like Theo Atrides wants his passing fancies to get pregnant? And that's all you are to him! Nothing more...

She stared out over the sunlit terrace. Paradise had just turned to ashes all around her.

* * *

Theo was not horrible to her—but he simply retreated into an impersonal, remote politeness that she could not break through. Not that she tried. She felt so guilty for having been so stupid, so irresponsible, that she could not blame him for the way he was behaving.

Only as he was about to leave did she catch at his sleeve and blurt out, 'Theo—my period—it's due in a couple of days. Please, please don't worry!'

He merely smiled briefly at her perfunctorily and excused himself, heading out to the helicopter.

It was a long, endless day. Leandra was filled with restlessness. As she paced the terrace, or tried to relax by swimming, she felt her tension mount like a clock spring. She missed him already. Missed his lovemaking, missed his laughter—missed *him*.

An ache opened up in her heart. *Come back to me! Oh, come back to me as quickly as you can!* After all, she thought with ruefully wanton desperation, he could easily buy condoms in Athens...

As the sun westered in the sky she took to the highest part of the island and scanned the horizon, straining her ears for the sound of rotors. As she sat and waited she thought of that first day she had sat in this same place, terrified out of her wits about what had happened to her.

Her life had changed totally since then. Turned upside down and inside out. Changed utterly.

She had fallen in love with Theo Atrides.

For she knew that that was what had happened. Knew that that was why she had gone to his arms, his bed, unable to deny the overwhelming feelings that had swept through her, blowing away all caution, all suspicion.

Oh, she knew he did not love her back! Knew that that was impossible. But for her the falling had been irreversible.

She would never stop loving him.

Her eyes went back to conning the skies.

But Theo Atrides did not come home that night.

Alone in his bed, Leandra tossed and turned, aching for his large warm body beside her, inside her...

She was sitting on the terrace the next morning, disconsolately reading one of the books Theo had found for her, when the sound of rotors came to her. Eagerly she rushed down to the landing pad, but when the helicopter landed the man who emerged was not Theo.

'Ms Ross—Mr Atrides requests that you return to Athens, if you please,' said the polite young man. He looked at her incuriously, Leandra realised, and with a flush she knew that he saw nothing unusual in his boss depositing or collecting bed mates from his private island.

In Athens, she was driven by chauffeured car through the teeming streets until they reached a quiet, but expensive part of the city. She looked about, hoping to see Theo, but the aide simply ushered her into a tall, anonymous building. It was, she swiftly realised, a private medical clinic.

A nurse came forward to greet her. She was polite, but unforthcoming. The doctor who saw her, however, was far more open. He made a complete internal examination of her, asked her detailed questions about her menstrual cycle and made notes. Then he smiled impersonally and handed her over to the nurse to perform a pregnancy test. Leandra tried to explain that it was far too soon for anything to register, but the nurse simply smiled and went ahead anyway. Leandra gave in.

Afterwards, she was conducted back to the waiting room, where Theo's aide was waiting. Politely he escorted her from the clinic, and took her to a large, luxurious and quite impersonal hotel in Athens.

'Mr Atrides will call on you later in the day. Please do not leave the hotel,' he instructed her politely, before departing.

It was as well she was warned, because otherwise Leandra would have plunged out into the streets of Athens, desperate to divert her mind from the brooding fears which had been growing ever since Theo had left her. As it was, cooped up

in the luxurious room, she had nothing to do but pace up
and down, idly flicking TV channels.

What was going on? *What was going on?*

Questions buzzed round her brain. Why had the nurse
taken a sample for a pregnancy test when surely nothing
could show this soon after making love? She had told them
her period was due soon, and her own familiar body changes
were affirming that. What worried her most, however, was
Theo's absence. She tried to be reasonable about it, remind-
ing herself that Theo Atrides was a captain of industry, that
he had a vast business empire to run, that men like him
worked long hours, with little time for romantic dalliance...
She must simply wait patiently until he could leave his office and come back to her.

And when he did she would be ready for him!

Eyes lighting in happy anticipation, she spent the next
couple of hours having a huge deep bubble bath and attending to a scrupulous beautifying programme. Shortly after she had been deposited in the hotel a bellboy had arrived
with a suitcase full of her clothes from the island, as well
as a vanity case containing everything she could possibly
need to make herself as lovely for Theo as she could.

As she stared at herself, wearing one of the beautiful silk
negligees Theo's PA had included in her purchases, her spirits recovered. Her golden hair, freshly washed and dried,
streamed down over her back. Her make-up was subtle, but
enhanced her natural beauty. Her body was soft and
creamed—and aching for Theo.

When he came she would beg his forgiveness for having
been so reckless, so thoughtless as to neglect contraception.
He would forgive her! Surely he would forgive her, understand that she had been so overwhelmed by his lovemaking
that it had driven out all thought of anything else!

And then, when that had all been sorted out, he would
smile at her again, and that troubled, brooding look would
leave his face and she would be his again—for as long as
he wanted her...

Because she wasn't pregnant—was sure she wasn't! Her body simply felt lush, and wanton, that was all.

And aching for his possession.

Impulsively, she ordered a bottle of champagne from Room Service, storing it in the mini-fridge in the room. She shaded the windows, drew back the bedcovers. Surely Theo would not be long now!

He came in the early evening. Leandra heard the card slice in the door lock and whirled around as the door opened. She stood, poised, and feasted her eyes on him.

Theo stood in the doorway, quite still. His eyes were locked on her. A nerve was ticking in his cheek. He looked as tense as a whip.

And sexy as hell.

She went towards him. She couldn't help it. She had been deprived of him for thirty-six hours and her starvation for him was absolute. She needed him—needed him now!

She pressed her body against his, glorying in the hard, solid feel of him, crushing up against him, winding her arms around his neck.

'Oh, Theo, I've missed you so much!' Her voice was a soft little cry. She lifted her mouth, to catch at his and feed on the sweetest nectar of his kiss.

His body stiffened, every muscle taut as a bow. Then, his hands closing on her arms like steel bands, he put her away from him.

'No, Leandra—don't touch me.'

His voice was heavy. She stood, eyes puzzled, anxious, not understanding.

He closed the door with a snap and walked across the room, increasing his distance from her. She stared after him, heart thumping. What was happening?

He enlightened her.

'It's no good, Leandra.' His voice was heavy still. 'Your tricks won't work any more.'

'Tricks?' she echoed faintly.

His eyes looked bleak suddenly.

'What else would you call them?' he intoned.

His face was shuttered, the way it had been when he had asked her about contraception the morning he had flown back to Athens.

'Perhaps,' he went on in that same flat voice, 'you might call them an insurance policy. A meal ticket, perhaps. A golden one. For life.'

Consternation filled her.

'Theo—please—what are you saying? I don't understand! Look, if you are angry or upset about my being stupid enough not to think about contraception, then I'm sorry—I truly am! It was rash and foolish of me, I know. But…well—' she tried to smile, but it didn't work somehow '—I was just too carried away to think about it.' She made another attempt at a smile, but that didn't work either. 'You made me forget about everything—except you, Theo…'

Her voice trailed off. His face was still closed, impenetrable. He looked older, suddenly, she realised, as if the weight of the world were on him. Nervously she twisted her hands together.

He saw the gesture, and the bleakness in his eyes intensified.

'Leandra,' he said heavily, 'if it had been just the first time I might, *might* have believed you! I might just have thought that, yes, contraception was the last thing you were thinking about. God knows,' he said with mordant self-accusation, 'it was the last thing I was thinking about!'

He took a breath that sounded painful in his throat. 'But you cannot stand there and tell me that for two days you just "didn't think" about contraception. We made love so often that you *must* then have given it some thought! It was obvious to you by then that I was not taking any precautions—if you were similarly unprotected why did you not say something? As for me—' his voice flattened even more, and a bitter, yet more self-accusing note entered it '—knowing that you were Demos's mistress, and that he must therefore have checked you were clean, gave me a sense of liberation I could not resist! I indulged myself in naked sex with you because I trusted you, Leandra. I trusted you.'

His eyes slid over her. Seeing her body—but nothing else. 'And you betrayed me.'

A cry of rejection escaped her. He ignored it.

'You cannot seriously expect me to believe that for two days you "forgot" about contraception—and that means—' his eyes hardened '—there is only one explanation for your silence on the matter. It was deliberate. You deliberately indulged in unprotected sex with me.'

She shook her head. 'No! No, Theo—I didn't—truly, I didn't!'

He slashed his hand in impatience. 'Leandra—you are not some naïve teenager! You are a very sexually experienced woman! You have been my cousin's mistress! Of course you knew what you were doing! You wanted me to think— as I did—that you were on the Pill. What else should I think of a woman who had been living with Demos for weeks? And what should I think of you now but that you deceived me deliberately?'

'No,' she said faintly, so faintly.

She couldn't believe this was happening. Couldn't believe that a simple, stupid mistake was having such a terrible effect.

Theo was talking again. His voice was like stone. Condemning her.

'And to what end, Leandra, would you have deceived me in such a fashion? Why would you deliberately indulge in unprotected sex with me? I can think of two reasons—and both are unforgivable.'

His dark eyes looked across at her. Repulsing her.

'You were either pregnant already—or hoping to become so.'

A gasp escaped her. She shook her head in instant denial. 'No! No, Theo!'

A rasp sounded in his throat. 'Well, on the first count you have been discharged. The doctor at the clinic you visited today assures me you are not pregnant. So—' his mouth twisted '—it seems that you are not already carrying Demos's child, as I at first suspected.'

She stared at him disbelievingly. 'Demos's child?' she echoed faintly. Was *that* what he had feared? Was *that* why the clinic had done a pregnancy test on her today?

He shrugged. 'Yes, why not? That could have been your plan all along. Who knows? Getting pregnant by Demos would have stopped his engagement in its tracks and given you a wealthy man to look after you financially all your life. Of course—' his voice hardened again '—when your liaison with my cousin was so abruptly ended, and you realised that his engagement to Sofia Allessandros was only a matter of time, you might well have decided that I would be quite adequate as a substitute father! The blood relationship is close enough for you easily to pass off Demos's child as mine, and certainly I am even richer than he is!'

Leandra's mouth was dry as dust. What he was telling her was appalling! He could not believe it—surely he could not? Dismay filled her. She tried to speak, but he went on in the same dispassionate tones that chilled her more than anything else.

'But it seems you are not pregnant by Demos, so that, at least, I must be grateful for. Now all I have to do is wait and see if a fate almost as bad awaits me. Fathering a child on you myself.'

She flinched as if he had struck her. He saw her recoil and smiled thinly. There was not a trace of humour in it.

'Oh, don't look anxious! There is no need! For if you are indeed pregnant, Leandra, then you will have your golden meal ticket for life, never fear! No child of mine will be rejected, or born illegitimate—whatever I think of its mother! Any such child will be secure, and safe, and loved by me! So I will marry you, be assured. And as my wife, the mother of my child, you will in live in luxury all your days. There—is that not a pleasing prospect for you?'

She paled. It was a hideous prospect—hideous! To be

married to Theo because he had no other option, simply because he felt he must do his duty by a child he had never wanted, never intended to conceive, was anathema!

She shook her head. It would never happen. She had already, in the long, long hours of his absence, made her mind up on that. If she were indeed pregnant, if her own rash foolishness had resulted in a baby, then she would make no claims on Theo whatsoever. She would go back to England and bear the child on her own, be a single mother. Oh, it would be difficult, but she would manage. Her career would have to go, but that was no matter. She had her parents' house by the sea to live in—she would do bed-and-breakfast in the summer, take in lodgers in the winter. She would get by. And she would never see Theo Atrides again. Her heart squeezed. After all, it was not as if she was going to see him once he had tired of her, once the novelty of bedding her had worn off. She did not fool herself she meant anything to him...

She would not have Theo—whatever happened she would never have Theo—but she would have his child...

Longing, sweet and piercing, rushed through her as she thought of holding Theo's child in her arms...

His words cut through her reverie. They were crisp and businesslike. Chilling her with their deadly dispassion.

'If your period is late, then you will have another pregnancy test immediately afterwards. If the result is positive we shall be married without delay.' His mouth twisted again. 'I did not think that I would beat Demos to the altar—and with such a bride at my side.'

She flinched again, at the cold derision in his voice. She had to make him see that he was wrong! Completely wrong! That she had never deliberately courted pregnancy!

She took a step towards him, face working.

'Theo, please, please believe it was nothing more than an accident! Forgetting about contraception!'

His lip curled.

'An accident? No, I think not. I know the ways of ambitious women better than you think, Leandra. Why do you think I have confined myself to women who are rich in their own right?' He lifted an eyebrow. 'Do you think you are the first to use her womb in a moneymaking scheme to enrich herself at the expense of the Atrides wealth?'

His voice sounded hollow.

'But you were certainly the cleverest. I grant you that. Oh, I grant you that.'

He looked at her across the room, across a gulf so wide she knew now, with a blooming of bitter despair in her heart, that it could never be breached. That it was so wide it had swallowed up everything that had flowered between them, so gloriously—so briefly.

Nothing was left.

He was talking still, and the words came like knife-cuts at her.

'Like all cheats, you played on my weaknesses, Leandra. You realised I despised you as a woman who chooses her lovers for the size of their bank accounts, and realised that I would never bed such a woman. So you took on the mantle of a woman of virtue! You took a gamble, turning down a safe hundred thousand pounds to net a much bigger prize!'

His voice rose and fell in those dispassionate, deadly tones, and Leandra stood there, letting it wash over her like a tide of coruscating acid, eating away at something so precious she felt a physical pain as it was destroyed in front of her eyes.

'And then you played the same hand all over again, with the diamond necklace. That time it was tears, not rage, that you turned on for my benefit. And it worked, Leandra—oh, it worked! As did your indignation over the clothes I bought for you, and your oh-so-convincing reluctance to succumb to me! Yes, so clever, Leandra—playing me inch by inch, on your silken web, reeling me in…'

Her heart was like a stone, as heavy as lead.

He was speaking again, and she forced herself to listen. Her world was crashing down around her and she felt sick,

sick right into the very core of her, because everything had gone wrong, so hideously, hideously wrong.

'You had me running circles around you, confusing me, making me stupid, senseless with aching for you! Until I was besotted with you! Putty in your hands! Just the way you planned all along…'

His voice was coming from very far away now. The other side of the world.

'And once you had me in your trap you couldn't lose, could you Leandra? Whatever happened you profited! If you weren't pregnant—if I started taking precautions myself—then you would be my pampered mistress and I would shower my wealth upon you. And if it was your lucky day—or night—and you conceived, then your profit margin would be even greater! You would be financially secure for life even if I never married you. And if I did marry you—and there was a good chance I might, for did you not know that my grandfather was desperate for an heir? So what if it was his other grandson who provided it— Well, as Mrs Theo Atrides the world would be yours for the buying!'

His voice dropped. His eyes burned like cruel flames.

'Or did you have one final scheme in mind? One final pay-out?'

A rasp sounded in his throat like a knife-blade. His voice sank to a low, harsh thrust.

'Did you prefer to make your fortune without even losing that lush, luscious figure of yours, Leandra? Did you think you could hold out your hand for a cheque with enough zeroes on it to ensure that you took a trip to an abortion clinic…'

Faintness drummed at her. She pressed her hands to her ears to cut out the vileness of this last, most repulsive accusation.

'No!' Her voice tore from her throat. Denying everything he had said of her. 'No! Everything you've said! It's not true—none of it!'

Theo's face was like stone.

'None of it? So I'm imagining it, is that it? I'm imagining that you knowingly, deliberately, had unprotected sex with me, time after time… And never once, not *once* thought to mention the fact?'

The scorn in his voice was unconcealed.

She looked at him helplessly.

How could he have said such things to me? Accusing me of scheming to deceive him, get money from him! How could he even think them after all we have had together?

She searched his face, looking for the man who had opened heaven's gate to her. There was nothing there—no trace of the man she had given herself to so rapturously. No trace of the man who had possessed her in the fires of passion. No trace of the man who had held her in his arms, against his heart…

Just a stranger. Worse than a stranger.

Something died inside her. Withered and died.

She stood, head bowed, defeated.

'It wasn't like that, Theo—truly to God it wasn't.'

It was all she could say, the only truth she could cling to as her world crashed around her. But it was not enough.

He made a noise in his throat and shook his head.

'It doesn't matter, Leandra. None of this matters any more. Only one thing matters—are you or are you not carrying my child? That is all I need to know. Nothing else.'

He looked at his watch. She saw the sleeve of his jacket ride back, saw the strong, powerful twist of his wrist. Felt the weakness go through her as her body yearned for his.

His mouth tightened.

'I must leave you now. I have a business engagement for dinner.' He spoke in distant, dispassionate tones. 'Tomorrow I must fly to Milan. I will be there several days. If your period has not arrived by the time I return I will accompany you to the clinic for a pregnancy test, and then—' his breath inhaled sharply '—we shall take it from there.'

He glanced around. 'You are comfortable here? You have everything you want?'

His voice was courteous—as courteous as a complete stranger.

She nodded, unable to say anything. But what was there to say? Nothing—there was nothing to say to Theo Atrides. Ever again.

'Good,' he acknowledged. 'Very well, I shall take my leave. If you wish to sightsee a car will be at your disposal. Your passport has arrived, but if you don't mind I shall keep it until we know the results of your pregnancy test. Please do not attempt to leave Athens, Leandra—I do not want to waste my time tracking you down. As for Demos—' his voice hardened '—I ask you not to contact him. My grandfather is still with him, and his PA has instructions not to put you through if you phone his office. His life is complicated enough as it is without your plaguing him again.'

He took another sharp inhalation of breath. 'I think that is everything. I will bid you good evening.'

He walked past her. As he did so she caught a faint, elusive scent of aftershave, of the scent of his own, masculine body. He did not touch her. He did not look at her. He simply left.

In the silence after the door had closed behind him, in the emptiness of her room, in the emptiness of her life, slow tears started to seep from her eyes.

The lift doors closed on Theo. Claustrophobia clawed at him. He felt crushed, annihilated. What a fool he had been! What a stupid, unforgivable fool! He had thought he had found paradise—it had been a mirage.

Just like before.

Deceived. He had been deceived! Putting his trust in a woman—like a fool. Just as he had been before! Like time rolling back he felt again the shock and the pain of that first time. He had thought Leandra, who had delighted him, captivated him beyond all reason, all expectation, was nothing like that other one...

She was exactly the same! False. Totally false.

She had denied all his accusations, looked stricken as he'd thrown them at her—even that last, most terrible one—but so what? She was a clever woman—knowing how to appeal to what he wanted to find in her! Knowing how to pretend to be the woman he had been so overjoyed to find! So exultant at possessing! But he would not be taken in again by her. Never again. From the moment when, lying with her in his arms, his guts had turned to ice as the realisation had dawned on him that he had just spent two days in rapture with a woman who had deliberately, knowingly, had unprotected sex with him, from that bleak, unforgiving moment the scales had been ripped agonisingly from his eyes. He could see through her now—see every twist and turn she had made to fool him! Her deceits were over...

And so was the happiness he had found with her—that searing, burning, liberating happiness that had cut the chains of the past, opening a future to him that he had never thought he could have...

Illusions! More illusions! He must rip them from him mercilessly, ruthlessly.

Or they would destroy him.

Darkness closed in on him. Blinding him to everything—everything but the nightmare that was consuming him, taking away all that he had once thought he had. Leeching out the happiness he had found with her, draining it from him, hour after hour, until there was nothing left. While he prayed, prayed desperately that there might be some reason, some totally innocent reason, for why Leandra had not told him she was unprotected.

But no innocent reason existed. Only a guilty one.

She had done it on purpose, as a means to extract money from him.

I should have known that a woman who had already been the mistress of one rich man would do anything to enrich herself at the expense of another!

Pain seared at him. More than pain. Despair.

The lift moved down. Towards hell.

*   *   *

Three days later Leandra knew she was not pregnant. She phoned the clinic, as she had been instructed to do, and dully relayed the information. An hour later one of Theo's aides arrived to conduct her to the clinic—the doctor, she presumed, was under strict instructions to check out her claim personally. Her word alone was not good enough.

When it was all over she sat in the waiting room. She stared at the walls. She was numb, totally numb.

After a while Theo arrived.

Seeing him was like a stab to the heart. She did not move.

He spoke with difficulty. 'I understand you are not pregnant.'

She nodded briefly, saying nothing.

He seemed ill at ease, restless. She watched him from very far away.

There was something in his eyes that hurt her.

'Well—very well,' he began. He paused, then looked at her. He took a breath. 'Leandra—'

'I want to go home!' Her words burst from her, sharp and staccato.

He stilled.

'Right now! Today! Give me back my passport! I'll take a taxi to the airport and fly out on the next flight! You can't keep me here any longer—you can't!'

Something flickered in his face. It might have been pain. She didn't know. She didn't care.

'I want out, Theo! Out right now!'

Her voice had risen. Pressure had forced it higher. There was pressure in her whole body, squeezing her, crushing her from the inside.

'Leandra—'

She stood up, silencing him. 'No! I don't want to hear anything else you have to say! Nothing! You've made your opinion of me crystal-clear! And now I've spared you the onerous task of marrying me I don't have to stick around any longer! So I want out, right now!'

He frowned. 'Where will you go? You cannot go back to Demos!'

A hiss sounded from between her teeth. 'Oh, don't worry! He's safe from me!'

For a moment, a brief, vicious moment, she wanted to throw the truth at his head! To tell him that his precious cousin had always been safe from her! Hope flared in her. Raw, desperate hope. If she could tell Theo that Demos had never been her lover then perhaps she could convince him he had no right to throw any of those vile accusations at her!

But even as hope flared it died. Extinguished by a truth she could not deny. So what if she had never been a rich man's mistress? She was still guilty of a crime that condemned her in Theo's eyes, that turned her instantly into the scheming, deceitful female he thought her. A crime that damned her totally—being so reckless, so irresponsible as not to worry about contraception when he had swept her into his arms, his bed. How could she ever prove to Theo she had not hoped to conceive his child, to get some kind of hold over him by which to extract his precious wealth from him? An impecunious actress, she thought with slicing bitterness, was just the kind to want to enrich herself at the expense of a passing Greek millionaire who fancied her in his bed...

And what if she told him that other truth? The one she had been denying even to herself but which had welled up in her hour by hour, day by day, in Theo's arms, in paradise? That lost, poisoned paradise.

The truth that now stabbed as cruelly as an assassin's knife in her side, piercing her very heart.

What if she told him that she had fallen in love with him? That she had committed the unspeakable folly of falling in love with a man who stood there, accusing and condemning, and to whom she could never plead her innocence.

She did not even have to think to answer. He would simply think it one more scheme to make money out of him.

As if he had read her thoughts, he spoke again.

'If you need funds—' he began.

Her face set stormily. 'No, thank you,' she clipped out viciously, cutting him off.

His wealth had destroyed everything that had been between them.

His voice was heavy. 'I will, of course, see to the expense of your return flight to London.'

'Don't bother!'

His eyes flashed. 'It was not, I believe, your fault that you ended up here in Greece. Therefore it is the responsibility of the Atrides to return you at no cost to yourself.'

She closed her eyes. 'I don't care. Just get me out of here. Just let me go home. Let me go home.'

She looked so defeated. So broken. For a moment, a long, terrible moment, Theo wondered if he had been wrong about her.

Then he hardened his heart. This was a woman who had clung to his cousin's arm like a limpet, who had worn his cousin's diamonds, warmed his bed. Oh, she might look like innocence personified, like a golden-haired nymph of the sea, but he knew better now! Oh, he knew better. It was all an act, nothing but an act!

Money shows their true colours!

His grandfather's words burned like acid. Some women, like this one now, were too cunning to be caught in so simple a snare. They played for higher stakes. Played on the hapless emotions of the men they caught in their toils…

Made fools of them.

'Very well.' His voice came brusquely. 'You can go home. You can do whatever you want. Be whatever you want. Catch another besotted, gullible fool with your beauty and your cunning. As for me—' his voice twisted and broke '—I wish to God I had never laid eyes on you!'

Leandra stared blindly out over the rooftops of south London. Theo had not come near her again, leaving it to his aide to collect her from the clinic and take her to the airport, where her passport and airline ticket had been waiting for her.

Demos and Chris had met her in London, taken one look at her ravaged face and exchanged appalled looks.

'What did Theo do to you, Lea?' Chris asked in low tones, taking her hand. Her fingers clutched his desperately.

Demos knew his cousin. Knew him all too well. *Trust me*, Theo had said to Demos.

Trust him to do what?

'If he has dishonoured you,' he said to Leandra, sitting at her side in the huge limo, 'he will marry you. I promise you that!'

A shudder jarred through her and she gave a stifled, frightened cry.

Chris and Demos exchanged worried glances again.

'Please,' Leandra begged in a strained voice, 'just take me home! Take me home!'

After the opulence of Demos's Mayfair apartment, and the rustic beauty of the island, her studio flat seemed bleak and drear. It suited her mood.

Unrequited love. The phrase seared in Leandra's head. What a joke! What a vicious, agonising joke! It had always seemed such a romantic condition. Poignant. Soulful. The traditional fate of every heroine in drama. In reality it was nothing like that. It was a tearing, ugly agony, more cruel than Medea's poisoned cloak, lacerating her body, her heart. Day after agonising day. Week after agonising week.

A wound that could never heal...

Work was her salvation. Her hold on sanity. The rehearsals for the Marchester Festival had started, and were extremely mentally demanding. Leandra could only be grateful, for her absorption into her difficult role helped to block out her own raw, bleeding emotions over Theo Atrides.

She was trying to pull the gaping edges of her shattered heart together and get on with life.

Even if she felt that her life was over—that the pain would never leave her.

The world was empty without Theo Atrides in it. And he was gone from her for ever.

Only in her dreams could she possess him still—but they were torture to endure. In her dreams, alone in her bed, Theo's presence filled her, body and soul, and in her dreams she relived, over and over again, the incandescent rapture of their union, so that morning after morning she woke with her cheeks wet with tears shed for what she had lost.

One other bitter pill she was forced to swallow: Theo Atrides had washed her out of his life like dirt on his hands.

He had moved on to pastures new.

Leandra had to watch, in a blaze of publicity, one of the world's great solo artists, Diana Delado, parading Theo Atrides on her arm, certainly as her lover, even perhaps—so the columnists speculated wildly—her next prospective husband. A scandalous liaison with a prominent and very married US senator had ensured that whatever Diana Delado did—and especially whoever she did it with—was hot news on both sides of the Atlantic.

As autumn slipped into winter, Leandra had to endure seeing pictures of the stunning, sultry singer accessorised by the man who had, a lifetime ago, taken her to her own private Eden. Before proving himself the serpent in its midst.

Leandra found one picture of them inside a glossy celebrity magazine that encapsulated all the heartache she was enduring. Side by side on the steps of the casino in Monte Carlo stood Diana Delado in glittering evening dress and Theo, dazzling in a tuxedo. He was smiling down at the petite singer, who was looking out of the photo. The sight of Theo's dark, glossy head, his strong features and the lazily amused smile on his sensuous lips, all turned knives in Leandra's heart. She stared at it a full moment, then carefully cut out the picture, pinning it to the inside of her ward-

robe door. From time to time she would open the door, stare
at the photo and remember what he had done to her.

Then, slowly, she would close it again and get on with
her life.

The first night of the Marchester Festival arrived. Chris and
Demos were there to see her. Though both of them were
still concerned about her, blaming themselves for ever having involved her so disastrously in their scheme to prevent
Demos's betrothal to Sofia Allessandros, she had seen little
of them since coming back to London for they were an
agonising reminder of Theo Atrides.

But it was good to see them again as they came to wish
her luck before the performance. She hugged them both.

'I have some news,' said Demos, watching Leandra carefully. 'Sofia Allessandros has become engaged to someone
else. She has washed her hands of me. I believe,' he said
cautiously, 'she is very happy with her father's new choice.
He lives in Athens, and I know she never wanted to move
to London.'

Leandra smiled. 'I'm glad it has worked out for her. And
for you, Demos.'

Demos was still looking at her. 'I wanted to thank you
again, Leandra, from the bottom of my heart, for your kindness to me.'

She shook her head. 'It was nothing.'

'No,' he disagreed. 'It was not nothing. I know the price
you paid for helping me.'

His dark, kind eyes rested on her, so like his cousin's.
But Theo had never looked at her with such kindess...

Her heart constricted.

'It wasn't your fault, Demos. It was my own.'

'Demos wants to tell Theo that it was all just a charade
between you,' said Chris.

Her eyes flared. 'There's no point,' she said bleakly. 'It
doesn't matter what he thinks of me.'

Behind her head Chris and Demos exchanged glances.

'Theo has not been himself, Leandra,' said Demos slowly.
'These past weeks he has been...different. He stopped off

in London on his way to New York—he wanted...' He
paused, his eyes on Leandra. 'He wanted to know if you
were back with me again. I told him no. He looked...
relieved.'

She gave a shrug. 'He would. After all, separating me
from you was what it was all about, wasn't it?' Bitterness
crept into her voice. She wanted them to stop talking about
Theo. Wanted never to hear his name again.

Abruptly she changed the subject.

'Is your grandfather very upset, Demos? About Sofia marrying someone else?'

Demos accepted the diversion. He had seen the pain flare
in Leandra's eyes when he spoke of his cousin.

'I feel bad,' admitted Demos, 'but what can I do? I can
never give him the heir he craves.'

Anguish flooded through Leandra at his words.

*I might have done that...I could have given him the heir
he wants so desperately!*

Then icy water deluged her heart. She could hear Theo
denounce her all over again...

Once more she changed the subject deliberately—to
something Theo Atrides had nothing to do with at all.

'I want to thank you again, Demos, for all the coaching
you gave me for my part. I could never have learnt it without you!'

He laughed self-deprecatingly. 'I am happy to have
helped—and I wish you the very best fortune for tonight.'

'Knock 'em dead, Lea,' said Chris cheerfully, getting to
his feet with Demos and preparing to leave her to get ready
for the performance. 'It's not my thing—but slay 'em, all
the same!'

Both congratulated her—and all the cast—hugely when
the performance ended. Leandra felt drained—it was an ex-
hausting role, mentally and emotionally. But she was filled
with the glow that always came at the end of a good performance, and her mood had lifted dramatically. Her hard
work had paid off and the production was deemed a success.

The cast and highly specialised audience unwound in a refined celebration afterwards. As first-night parties went it was very sedate, so much so that at the close Leandra happily went off with Chris and Demos, ending up in Demos's suite at the best hotel in town. Demos produced champagne, and by the time it was finished Leandra was happy to crash out on the sofa in the sitting room, with empty champagne glasses on the coffee table in front of it. Chris laughed, tossed a spare blanket from the bedroom over her, and let her be.

She surfaced, late and bleary, the next morning, still buoyed up. The sheer exhilarating pleasure of having given a good performance, and in such a difficult role, was like a rush of endorphins through her, for once smothering the clawing pain that she woke to every morning when her fervid, frantic dreams of Theo Atrides—dreams in which she relived over and over again the erotic bliss of their congress, where he gazed down into her eyes with tenderness, cherishing and, most unreal of all, a blaze of love—gave way to harsh cruel reality.

She stood up, pushing her hair back off her face, and grimaced because she was still wearing the jade-green evening trouser suit she'd slept in, sadly crumpled after a night on the sofa. No, she told herself decisively, stretching her limbs and blinking to clear her head, don't think about him. Think about last night—tonight, the night after. Your performance is all—your art is all. Dedicate yourself to your art, and that alone.

It's all you have left...

A shower revitalised her, and half an hour later she was curled up on the end of Demos's bed finishing a hearty breakfast. She was wearing a hotel bathrobe and her loose hair streamed down her back. Demos, looking very elegant in monogrammed black silk pyjamas, was drinking coffee, propped up against the pillows.

'A pity there are no reviews,' he said to her. 'They would be glowing, I know!'

She laughed. 'The festival's far too small for that. The production might make the local paper next week, I suppose, if they're a bit short of news!' She gave a languorous stretch. 'I must head off—if the rest of the cast discover I've spent the night in a luxury hotel instead of in the hostel with them I'll be lynched!'

She set the tray down on the floor and was just about to rebelt her robe, which had fallen loose across her breasts, when there came the sound of the outer door to the hotel corridor opening sharply into the suite's sitting room. She paused, glancing at Demos.

'More Room Service?'

'I didn't order anything—' he began, mystified.

The door to the bedroom was flung open. An instant later the tall, commanding figure of Theo Atrides stood framed in the doorway, tension in every long line of his body.

CHAPTER TEN

FOR a moment nobody moved, frozen into a tableau. Then, in a hard, curt voice, Theo Atrides spoke. Not to his cousin, who was staring at him transfixed, but to Leandra.

'Get dressed.'

His voice was terse, and seemed to be strung like wire about to snap. His dark eyes bored into her like a drill.

She stared, wordless. Her heart was hammering inside her chest—she felt bereft of breath. A mix of fear and—far, far worse—searing, incandescent joy at seeing him again soared through her.

'Get dressed,' he ordered brusquely again. 'We're going.'

His words made no sense. She went on staring—drinking him in—drinking in the long, lean, powerful body, the dark crisp hair, the hooded eyes and that wide, sensual mouth, set now like steel between the deep lines carved from the base of his nose.

It was Demos who recovered first. 'What the hell do you think you're doing here—?' he began.

His cousin cut him short. Swiftly, ruthlessly.

'I'm taking Leandra,' he said roughly. 'She's mine—not yours. She always will be. I want her and I'll take her. She's not going back to you! Never!'

His eyes went to Leandra, his expression devouring. She went on clutching her bathrobe, incapable of speech, incapable of thought, just staring, helplessly, hopelessly. Heart hammering.

He gave a harsh laugh and advanced towards her. He stood in front of her.

'I want you back,' he told her simply. 'I cannot be without you. Not one more day without you. You will have all

159

the luxury you crave—all my wealth to spend! My Leandra—'

Numbly, as if she had no will of her own, she let his hands close around her upper arms and draw her to her feet. His closeness, his male scent, made her bones weak.

'Theo—I—' Her voice was a thread.

The bathroom door snapped open. A new figure appeared in the bedroom. Blond, impossibly handsome, wearing nothing but a towel wrapped around narrow hips, his bare, smooth chest still damp from his shower.

'What the hell—?' said Chris, joining the frozen tableau staring at Theo Atrides.

As his head whipped round and his eyes focused on the semi-naked young man emerging from the bathroom Theo Atrides stilled. Like stone. Leandra's faint breath caught in her throat, and closed it tight. She had seen that expression only once before on Theo Atrides' face—the moment he realised she had used no contraception.

For a long, timeless moment the man who had taken her to heaven and left her in hell stared at Chris. Then his eyes slid back to Leandra, via Demos, sitting in bed wearing his black silk pyjamas. Theo's hands slipped from her arms and he stood back, as if in the presence of something loathsome.

Something moved in his eyes. Moved, and died.

A word crawled from him. She did not understand it, but the way he said it made her blench. Demos understood it, and gave a shocked inhalation of breath.

Theo ignored him. He ignored Leandra. His eyes glanced from the half-naked blond man by the bathroom door to the dark-haired man in the bed. His lips twisted. It might have been a smile. But it was not. He looked back at Leandra.

His expression could have obliterated her on the spot.

'And to think,' he said slowly, as if every word were coated in foul slime, 'I once thought to reassure you that I had no taste for perversion!' His mouth twisted in revulsion. 'No wonder you did not answer me! I thought you shocked...'

His eyes dragged from her, dragged to the two men still staring horrified at him.

'And all along...'

He trailed into silence, then, with an odd, choking sound in his throat, he slammed from the room.

For an eternity, it seemed, the tableau in the bedroom held. Then, like a wash of acid through her, Leandra felt hot, burning colour stain her skin from toes to forehead.

'Lea—did he just say...?' Chris's voice was a croak of disbelief.

Behind her she could hear Demos suddenly spring out of bed, Greek spouting furiously from him.

She was galvanised, shooting to her feet, launching herself towards the door.

'Lea!' croaked Chris again, alarm in his voice now. 'Don't! Leave him to us! Leave him to—'

It was too late. She had wrenched the door open and erupted into the sitting room like an avenging angel.

'Don't you *dare* walk out of this room!' Her voice was a scream of white-hot fury.

At the door to the corridor Theo Atrides froze, hand on the handle. His body tautened. He did not turn around.

'Don't speak a word, Leandra—not one word,' he said in a voice so soft, so quiet—so cruel—it slayed her where she stood. 'I would strangle you with my bare hands if touching your depraved flesh would not soil them!'

With a little cry she snatched up an empty champagne glass and hurled it at his back. It bounced off, breaking as it landed on the floor. His shoulders tensed, but he did not turn, merely exerting pressure on the handle to open the door and walk out on her—the woman he had just accused of taking two men to her bed at the same time.

'Turn round and face me, you disgusting, vile-minded bastard!' Leandra screamed at him, hurling another champagne glass at him. It caught his shoulder this time, shattering on impact.

He whirled round, face contorted.

'How dare you?' she lashed at him. '*How dare you?* How dare you even *think* what you just said—let alone say it to my face? You have the vilest mind of anyone I know! You know nothing—*nothing!*'

His lips twisted. 'The evidence speaks for itself, *pethi mou.* One woman—one bed—two men. With all three of you—how shall I put it?—in *dishabille.*' His voice dripped contempt. More than contempt. Utter disgust. 'And to think I had come to believe that it was Demos who had led *you* astray. He is an innocent compared with you! Tell me— were you playing your little threesome party tricks with Demos and that blond hunk before or after you opened your legs for me?' His words, his voice, flayed the skin from her flesh. His eyes burnt into hers like hot irons branding her. 'I'm sorry I was so boring for you—if I'd known your tastes I'd have had some handsome young men flown in for you, to keep you happy. But you'd have had to count me out, I'm afraid. Not my scene.'

He turned to go again. She hurled the last glass at him. It missed, and smashed on the wall beside him. He gave an exaggerated flinch and opened the door.

'Go back to my cousin's bed, Leandra—he may enjoy your perversions. I don't. You sicken me. You all sicken me.'

His voice was flat. Final.

Rage convulsed her. The words hurled from her throat. 'I have *never* been in your cousin's bed! I have never been his *lover!* I have never slept with him *or* Chris! Neither of them would damn well want me! They're sleeping with each other, you moron!' Her breath caught, choking in her throat. 'That's why Demos could never marry Sofia! He's gay— he's in love with Chris—and this is such a God-awful, hideous mess I...I...' Her voice shook and her hands moved helplessly, hopelessly.

Then, with a cry that broke from her heart, she turned

and belted back into the bedroom, rushing through into the bathroom and slamming the door shut. She locked it against all the world. For ever.

The bar in the hotel was empty, all except one small table, tucked right away at the back. Even the barman had made a discreet withdrawal. At the table, two men sat. One was hunched over a glass of neat single malt whisky. The bottle, more than half empty, stood on the table beside it. It was mid-afternoon.

'What am I going to do?' asked the man clutching the whisky glass within the cage of his strong, long fingers. 'What the *hell* am I going to do, little cousin?'

He spoke Greek, and his voice was slurred. The whisky might have done it, but it was not the only cause. Demos opened his mouth to answer, but Theo just went on talking.

'I've screwed up everything. *Everything!* Dear God, how could I have got it so wrong? Got *her* so wrong! So totally, completely wrong! I've fouled up everything—all down the line!'

'Yes,' said Demos.

Theo lifted bleared eyes, wanting to kill the man who'd just agreed with him. Then his expression shifted. He looked haunted. Haggard.

'How?' he asked his cousin. 'How could I get it so wrong?'

'Because you thought the worst of her. Judged and condemned her. Every time,' said Demos. He had no mercy in his voice. He knew how deep a wound Theo had inflicted on Leandra. He'd seen it in her anguished eyes.

Theo's head lifted sharply. He came back fighting. '*Christos,* you wanted me to think she was your mistress! Clinging on to you! Wearing your diamonds! Nothing but a bimbo airhead hanging on to you for your money!'

Demos shrugged—a little uncomfortably, to be sure. 'Leandra's an actress, Theo. She was just acting a part! That wasn't the real her.'

Theo Atrides fought back again, like a drowning man.

'Did you pay her?' he demanded aggressively. 'Did you pay her to act as your mistress? Did she take your money for that?'

For a moment he thought his placid younger cousin would strike him. Then Demos controlled himself.

'No,' he said levelly, 'I did not pay her to act my mistress. She did it out of kindness. She's known…Chris…' he hesitated only slightly over his lover's name '…for years. They've been friends since drama school. When he told her of our…predicament she agreed to help out. I wish to God,' he said, suddenly savage, 'I'd never sucked her into this.'

His soft eyes flashed angrily. 'When Milo lost his head and abducted her you told me I could trust you, Theo—and I did! I trusted you! And what did you do?' His voice was condemning. 'You seduced her! I should have known, Theo! Known what you were capable of!' His voice was grim. 'I told her I'd make you marry her for dishonouring her! She looked petrified at the thought, but I swear to God, Theo, if she even once says yes, then you'll marry her! You'll marry her if I have to hold a gun to your head myself!'

There was a long silence. Theo's dark, shadowed eyes shifted away, staring into the darkness that was in his soul.

'She'll never have me now. Not now. I've blown it. Totally blown it. For the rest of my life.' He picked up the whisky glass and downed its contents in one. Then he poured himself another, setting down the bottle with a crack on the surface of the table. He tried to look at his cousin, and failed. 'I've lost her,' he said, and his voice was as bleak as Arctic wastes. 'I love her and I've lost her.'

He picked up the glass and put it to his lips, to knock it back. It was taken suddenly from his hand. His head snapped up, a snarl on his face.

'No,' said Demos sharply, getting to his feet and removing the glass and the bottle. 'On your feet, Theo. On your feet. You're a self-pitying, undeserving piece of junk right now—but I'm family, and you're going to get another chance.' He yanked his cousin to his feet—no mean achievement, given his cousin's much heavier build and inert muscles. Ignoring Theo's slurred protests he said roughly, 'And don't think it's for your sake I'm doing this—it's not! It's for Leandra—I want her to have the pleasure of seeing you crawl!'

He got Theo to the lift and pushed him ungently inside. As they ascended Theo slumped back heavily against the wall, lost in whisky fumes and brooding thought, his face haggard and drawn. Suddenly he looked his cousin straight in the eyes, as if remembering something that had hitherto slipped his mind.

'Demos—why the hell didn't you just tell me you were gay?' His voice slurred again, incomprehension in it. 'Why all this garbage you handed out to me about a mistress?'

'You wanted me to marry Sofia, remember?' replied his cousin tightly.

'Well, not if you're gay, for God's sake!' Theo reacted explosively. He ran his hands through his thick black hair. He stilled a moment, and once more looked his cousin in the eyes. Right in the eyes. 'This guy you're in love with—Chris—tell me, little cousin, did it hurt when you fell for him?'

'Yes,' said Demos. 'But not any more. Now,' he said, looking at Theo with compassion for the first time, 'now we're the whole world to each other.'

Theo's face buckled.

The entrance to the Faulknerian Library in Marchester was via an imposing sweep of shallow steps leading through a Corinthian portico to an echoing lobby. George Augustus Faulkner had made a fortune in the sugar trade in the eighteenth century, and had bought himself respectability by making lavish endowments to Marchester's Institute of Arts and Mechanical Instruction. Now the Institute was the University of Marchester, and the grand neo-classical library one of its centrepieces.

'I don't believe this,' growled Theo Atrides in a low,

incredulous voice to his cousin as they ascended the flight of steps. 'You throw me under a cold shower to sober up, pour water down my throat and a ton of coffee, put me to bed like an infant to sleep off the whisky and then drag me out for *this?*'

'Atrides plc is the sponsor,' his cousin told him, unmoved by Theo's objections. 'I have a duty to show up—so do you.'

'I never chose to sponsor it!'

'No, I did. Marchester's reputation is second to none in the country. It was a good choice for us. You'll see.'

His cousin rolled his eyeballs. 'I can think of a hundred better ways of spending the evening!'

'Can you?' returned Demos, as they walked inside. 'Tough.'

His cousin made an indefinable noise in his throat. Demos continued to be unmoved.

Some ten minutes later, civilities over, they were seated in the small but perfect Oval Saloon, with its celebrated Adam ceiling. Theo Atrides leant back in his tiny gilt chair—excruciatingly uncomfortable for a man of his large frame—and looked forward to an evening of purgatory. Only courtesy for his hosts held the expression of intense boredom from his face.

'A bunch of English amateurs—wonderful!' He contented himself with muttering to his cousin out of the corner of his mouth as the proceedings started.

'Not all of them are amateurs,' said Demos cryptically.

The drama started.

For all his native Hellenic doubts about the ability of English actors to recreate the glories of the fifth-century Attic stage in the original tongue, Theo Atrides had to allow that the library's neo-classical setting was perfect for an indoor performance of the play. Besides, Sophocles's pitiless drama of the princess Antigone, so tragically caught between private and public responsibilities, torn between loyalty to her family or to her community, was as relevant today as when the play had first been performed under the bright Aegean sun so long ago. But as the traditionally masked character of the young Princess Antigone made her entrance, and began to speak the very words Sophocles had written over two millennia ago, Theo Atrides sat suddenly bolt upright in his chair.

'Tell me I'm dreaming,' he said to his cousin in a hollow voice.

'No,' said Demos quietly. 'It's Leandra playing Antigone.' He paused. 'She has a Classics degree from Marchester University and she was invited to take the part in this specialist production.'

'Oh, my God,' said Theo Atrides in a hollow voice, of the woman he'd once thought nothing more than a scheming, gold-digging, sexy, airhead bimbo.

'Shh!' said the man sitting behind them irritably— Leandra's old professor of Greek.

Demos hushed. He'd made his point.

Theo felt his guts kicked in. All over again.

It took every ounce of Leandra's professionalism to get through the performance. There was no formal stage, and if she'd wanted she could have taken three steps and touched Theo Atrides with her bare hand. Or thumped him from here to Christmas. Only the recollection of the expression on his face when he'd recognised her kept her from doing just that.

'Timeo Danaos?' she'd gritted inwardly, grateful for her stiff, concealing mask, remembering how Theo Atrides had assumed Demos must have taught her the phrase like a parrot, when she could have spouted whole stanzas of Virgil's *Aeneid* in the original Latin if she'd wanted to. *'I don't think so, chum!'*

As the performance proceeded towards its tragic climax she was intensely grateful that it required total concentration for her to act in a highly stylised fashion, speaking an antique, foreign language, and convey Antigone's agonising emotions as the tragedy unfolded and she obeyed her conscience at the price of her life.

By the end of the drama she felt drained. She was also filled with a sense of dread. She did not know why Demos had brought Theo here. Was it nothing more than a sense of corporate duty from the festival's sponsor? Demos had made no mention of it, but then, she acknowledged, he had been more concerned to assure her that neither he nor Chris were upset by her storming revelation that morning.

'We should have been brave and come out months ago,' Chris had said.

'We had no right to embroil you in our problems,' his lover had agreed.

Both of them had put their arms around Leandra, but neither had mentioned Theo's name to her.

Now he was here, not six feet from her.

She knew she had to face him. She could not throw the truth in his face, as she had done this morning in her furious rage, and not expect him to want answers.

As she changed out of costume, chatting quietly to the other cast members, she felt a shaft of guilt go through her. Merely to justify herself in Theo's eyes, and give free reign to her fury at his vile accusations, she had betrayed Demos and Chris. Despite their reassurances, what damage had she done to Demos's relationship with his cousin?

They might be sitting next to each other tonight, but was that just for public consumption? Could a man as rampantly macho as Theo Atrides ever tolerate a different orientation? He'd denounced her supposed sexual debauchery as perversion—would he be as ruthless towards his cousin?

Heart heavy, she bade goodnight to the rest of the cast, who were off to supper, telling them she might join them later. Then, clad in jeans and sweatshirt, hair in its customary plait, skin free of make-up, she went back out into the Oval Saloon.

It was deserted apart from Theo Atrides.

As she came in his head turned towards her. Instantly,

though she would have paid a million pounds for it not to be so, her bones felt weak as water just from seeing him again. Her breath caught in her throat.

He looked breathtaking. His face was shuttered, but the familiar strong planes and the dark hooded eyes and oh-so-sensual mouth made her breath catch. He was wearing a charcoal business suit, formal tie and pristine white shirt, a slim gold watch glinting on his strong wrist. His tall, lean body overwhelmed her. A terrible impulse to run to him, wrap her arms around his long length and never let him go for the rest of her life, made Leandra's limbs tremble with the ferocity of her urge.

The vivid, searing lines of the Greek poetess Sappho leapt in her mind—'"Fire runs like a thief in my veins..."'

She must have spoken them aloud, and in the original.

Theo's taut expression tensed even more as he heard the tongue of his ancestors on her lips once more.

'Even I know those lines—every Greek schoolchild does,' he said harshly. 'Why didn't you tell me, Leandra? You had chance enough to throw it in my face!'

'Throw what?' she returned, her voice faint, holding it steady by force of will alone. Half the distance of the room separated them. And much, much more.

His eyes darkened. 'That you were just acting a part!'

Her face tightened. 'I had no choice. I had to protect Demos.'

'You put me through purgatory, letting me think you were his mistress!' he threw at her. The stark outline of his face was gaunt, his voice bleak-edged, but she felt no pity for him. 'Letting me think you were the kind of woman who would—'

She didn't let him finish. 'I...*I* put you through purgatory? My God, Theo Atrides, you are beyond belief! After everything you said to me—every foul accusation you laid at my door—!' Taking a deep shuddering breath, she steadied herself. Her chin lifted. Her expression was glacial.

'For the record, Mr Atrides—' her words were chill, precise '—despite being an impecunious actress, I did not participate in unprotected sex with you in order to impregnate myself with your child so I could extract money from you in any of the vile ways you outlined for me in such detail. I was stupid, yes, careless, yes, in being reckless enough to have sex with you without proper precautions, but believe me, your precious money was the last thing I was thinking about at the time! And also for the record, Mr Atrides,' she went on remorselessly, watching his face whiten beneath its customary tan as he moved to say something back to her, 'I would not willingly bear a child to you if you went down on your knees and begged me to marry you! I couldn't think of a fate worse than marrying you! Even in exchange for the immense privilege—' her sarcasm slashed at him furiously '—of spending all your money!'

She took a deep shuddering breath. He started to try and say something, but she cut him short again, tossing her head up.

'And now that I've cleared up that little fact with you, I'll tell you right now that I am here for one reason and one reason only—to warn you to lay off Chris and Demos! They've had enough pressure on them and they are both good friends of mine—so don't even *think* of trying a replay of your charming tactic by offering Chris money to leave Demos!'

Theo's face darkened. 'I would not dream of doing so!'

'Why not?' Leandra threw back at him. 'You thought it a good enough way of getting rid of me when you thought I was sharing your cousin's bed! Why so squeamish just because Chris is a man? Or is it,' she bit, 'because you don't happen to want to go to bed with him?'

A hand slashed through the air. 'Enough!' said Theo Atrides. He strode towards her, emotion working in him powerfully. She backed away. He stopped dead. 'I don't,' he told Leandra, 'want to talk about Demos—or his lover, whoever he is providing it is not *you!* I only want to talk about us!'

Her mouth trembled. 'There is no us. There never was.'

'There was always an us,' said Theo quietly. His expression changed. 'There was an us from the moment I saw you pressing up against Demos in that sexy little black dress you were half hanging out of! If I hadn't believed you were my cousin's woman I'd have whisked you up to a hotel room and you'd have been in bed with me that same evening! I wouldn't have waited a day to take you, Leandra—not an hour...'

His voice had dropped, its timbre sending coils of debilitating weakness through her as those hooded eyes surveyed her. Memory flared in her—hot and humid—of that first electrifying encounter with him. He saw her remembering it, and something changed in his eyes. Something of their Arctic bleakness ebbed. He took a step towards her.

'I wanted you then, Leandra—and I didn't want Demos to have you. I told myself it was because he had to be free to marry Sofia, but even then I knew it was because I wanted you for myself. Only myself.'

His eyes were dark, desiring. Leandra's heart started to race—fire laced her veins. Oh, God, he was so dangerous, so deadly—if he moved now—if he simply closed the distance between them and took her in his arms—she'd melt over him, into him, under him. It didn't matter what he had said to her, what he had done to her... She was helpless to resist him.

Theo Atrides went on talking to her, and she drank it all in—his words, his voice, the vision of his irresistible body standing there a few steps away from her. So close.

'I thought it would be so simple. But instead you spat and raged and threw diamonds in my face! You fought me all down the line. You infuriated me, enraged me, exasperated me—until I realised...' his voice changed, took on a rueful, caressing note '...the real reason I didn't want you to fight me.'

He looked her in her eyes, and Leandra had the strangest feeling she was seeing right into him for the very first time.

'Not because I wanted you to submit to me—but because I wanted you to love me. As I...' He faltered, then went on. 'As I was starting to love you.'

His voice changed again. 'I have known many women, but none—not one—did for me what you did when I finally took you. It was passion, but it was more—something in you touched me in a way no woman has, no woman could. Something that could only ever be between you and me— that we had never shared with anyone else. And suddenly,' he went on, his voice strange, 'no other lover mattered— neither mine nor yours! I knew that what we had was for us alone. And I rejoiced! I knew then that I would keep you at my side, in my bed—in my life.' He looked at her, his eyes resting on her. 'You made me the emperor of the world, Leandra.'

His voice tightened, like a garrotte around her hopes. 'And then, just as I was yielding to my delight in you, everything was ripped from me! I discovered what a fool I had become! What a gullible, besotted fool! When I realised you had used no contraception I thought only one thing! I thought that despite everything we had been to each other it was all just a lie! That it had meant nothing to you— nothing at all! That all I was to you was a yet richer source of treasure. It wasn't me you wanted—just my wealth. And you were plotting to win yourself a rich prize from me by the deliberate, cold-blooded creation of an Atrides child.

'And so,' he finished, a deadly stillness about him, his voice an Arctic waste, 'I got rid of you.'

Leandra stood there, very still, every nerve and sinew motionless.

'Yes,' she whispered. It was a thread of sound. Inaudible. 'You got rid of me.'

He didn't hear her. He was locked in his own memories. His eyes were inward looking, and something in his face was so terrible it made her breath catch.

'When I sent you back to London I vowed, Leandra, never to think of you again. Never to remember you. To wipe you out of my life, my heart, my memory, as if you had never been. And it took me a long, long time to face up to why I so desperately needed to do so.' As he spoke his voice grated, drawing his own blood.

His eyes focused on hers, and for the first time she knew she could see the pain in them. Reflecting her own.

'I had fallen in love with you, and I thought you had betrayed me. Made a fool of me. I would not, could not forgive you that!'

A deep, shuddering breath went through him.

'I tried to forget you,' he said, his voice as quiet as a grave. 'But you would not let yourself be forgotten. You haunted me, Leandra. Haunted me by day and by night, giving me no peace. You invaded my dreams, tormented my waking hours with wanting you. Craving you. And gradually, day by day, night by night, I realised that whatever you were I wanted you back. I wanted to hate and despise you for what you were—what I thought you were—but I could not. I could only want you—all of you. Because I had no peace without you.

'A thousand memories assailed me—not just of your lovely, throbbing body spread for me, but more—much more. I saw you dance out on to the terrace in that yellow dress, your hair floating around you like a golden mist— you enchanted me! I saw you splashing in the waves, breasting the sea with your soft white breasts—you beguiled me! I heard your sweet laughter as I showed off to you, tossing pancakes in the air for your delight—you captivated me! I felt you cling to me in the aftermath of passion, trembling in my arms—you awed me with the intensity of your response. And I could not do without you any longer. Despite everything I still thought you, I could not do without you.'

He paused to take a long, heavy breath. 'When Demos told me you had left to go your own way I rejoiced! He had no hold over you—so I was free to claim you back. And then, yesterday, in Athens, Demos's PA, whom I had asked to keep me posted, phoned to tell me he was coming here to meet you. I flew to England at once and raced here, determined that you should not go back to him—that you should come to me! I came after you, to take you on any terms I could. And lost you all over again.'

He turned away. Something had broken in him. It hurt her unbearably to see it so.

'When I saw you in Demos's room I didn't care. I had taken you from him once and I would take you again. I knew that once I had you in my arms, my bed, burning for me alone, he would mean nothing to you! And I would forgive you everything! You were poor—it was natural you should want a rich man! I understood that—I excused it! I would make you my wife and you would be mine for ever! And I would shower you with my wealth and your craving for a golden meal ticket for life would be assuaged—you could get as pregnant as you liked and I would only rejoice!

'And then—' his voice tautened, like wire pulled beyond its breaking strain '—the bathroom door opened and another man walked in, and I realised my world had just ended.' He looked at her, straight in the eyes. 'I saw my illusions about you stripped to the bone all over again. I saw a woman who sees nothing vile in being the sexual toy of two men together! Such a woman could only sicken and revolt me. For such a woman there could be no excuses, no forgiveness. Her depravity was absolute.

'And so,' he echoed, 'I rejected you again. This time for ever.'

The silence stretched between them. Tangible. Unbearable.

When he spoke his voice was as bitter as gall.

'But the joke was on me, Leandra. And now you may laugh all you wish. For you have not been one—' he spelt it out heavily, each word weighing more than she could bear to hear '—not even one of all the things I thought you. Not one.'

He took a heavy breath that razored in his throat. 'I misjudged you totally, Leandra. Presumed the worst about you—always—about everything. From beginning to end. I was a fool, and worse. A thug—a brute.'

He turned and walked away from her. Not looking back. He reached the tall double doors to the saloon and took the gilt handles in his grip to open them.

'I'm paying the price for having done what I did to you, Leandra, for what I thought about you in my arrogant presumption which always looked for the worst in you—and found it! Well, the last of my illusions is stripped from me— the illusion that you could ever want me in your life after all I have done to you, said to you, accused you of! You can take pleasure, as Demos told me he wanted you to, in seeing me crawl to you. And you can have one last pleasure from me as well—I now look forward to the inestimable pain of loving a woman who can only think of me with loathing!'

He gave a long, shuddering sigh that racked his powerful body. Then, in a harsh, husked, low voice, proud head bowed, he said, 'Goodbye, Leandra. Take care of yourself. If you should ever have need of anything an Atrides can provide you must let me know. I have an eternal debt to pay you.'

He did not look back at her. He simply walked out of the room and was gone.

CHAPTER ELEVEN

THE low Aegean sun was dipping towards its winter horizon as the helicopter made its whirring way over the darkening waters. Theo's face was set. This was a journey he did not wish to make. There was no reason for such a trip—Demos hardly needed a personal guided tour over the island that his cousin was making over to him. Theo never wanted to set foot on it again. Going there would be an exquisite form of torture.

But Demos had been insistent, so Theo had steeled himself and climbed aboard, curtly telling his cousin to pilot the machine himself. Throughout the journey they did not speak. Theo flicked open his briefcase and buried himself in his work.

Work was the only salvation he could find, and then it was painfully inadequate. The raging pain within him would not be stilled, it ate at him like a cancer. It would get worse, too, Theo knew. It was nearly Christmas by the Latin calendar, and the thought of having to join the family for the orthodox celebrations early in the New Year was gruelling. Once, a lifetime ago, he had imagined the joy he would bring his ailing grandfather by presenting his own bride to him. Demos might never give Milo great-grandsons, but he, Theo, would instead!

But there would be no Atrides bride to lighten Milo's last months on earth. Or give meaning to his grandson's empty existence.

Theo went back to studying his business papers. Profit and loss.

But especially loss.

It was late afternoon by the time they landed. At least

they would not be able to stay long. Theo wanted this ordeal over and done with. With the light going, Demos wanted a tour of the island first. Morosely, Theo accompanied him. He tried hard not to look about him, to keep his mental eyes shut from his surroundings. But the memories came all the same.

Demos, damn his soul, seemed oblivious to his cousin's sombre, painful preoccupation, talking about banalities such as water supply and telecommunication links. His cousin made terse, minimal replies, staring out sightlessly over the choppy wave-tossed seas. Winter had come. For Theo, it would never be spring.

A thousand memories fought for entrance to his locked, unseeing mind. Memories of Leandra at his side, his arm around her shoulder as they strolled around his domain, their private Eden—then him turning her to him and kissing her.

Then their hurried, urgent return to the house—their bed. Their sensual, ecstatic coupling.

Pain stabbed him again. Worse than ever. His loss was unbearable. Exile from paradise.

As they approached the landscaped gardens the pain of loss got worse yet. He remembered Leandra sitting under the vine, sunning herself on the terrace. Leant back against the wall, face lifted to the starry heavens, legs hugging him, gasping as he emptied himself into her soft, shuddering body. Clinging to him, naked as he, as he held her against his heart. Beating so wildly—but only for her. Only for her.

But I didn't know it, he thought bleakly. I didn't know it until it was too late.

Too late. The worst words in the world.

He wondered where she was, the woman he had loved too late too win. That she was somewhere under the same sky that sheltered him upon the wide earth was his only comfort. How strange, he thought, that love does this to you. How powerful it is. The most powerful thing in the world.

Except grief. And loss.

Abruptly he realised that his footfall on the winding steps

leading down to the sheltered garden of the villa from the higher rough ground beyond was falling alone. He glanced back. There was no sign of Demos. Frowning, irritated by yet more delay, he turned to re-ascend the rise. Then, suddenly, he heard the distinctive ignition of the helicopter's engine and the noisy rotation of the rotors. A moment later he saw the machine lift off behind the villa, hover momentarily, then veer and head back across the sea.

Disbelief stunned him. What the hell was Demos playing at? Stranding him here! Didn't he know the motor boat wasn't moored here at this time of year and that Agathias and Yiorgos were at home with their family on the mainland? Face grim, stunned with anger, he headed down the steps towards the villa. Now he would have to get the generator working, power up his computer, get the telecom kit going and summon another chopper to lift him off.

If this was some kind of stupid joke that Demos was playing on him there'd be hell to pay!

As the sound of the helicopter's engine died away, echoing into the distance, the silence of the drear evening lapped around him again. Then, into the silence, there was a new sound—a slight click. He stopped dead. The glass doors to the sitting room opened.

A woman stepped through, on to the terrace, catching the last of the frail winter sunlight.

She was like a vision, a dream. A mirage of lost happiness. Her dress was black velvet, sweeping in a bell down to the ground. From the night-dark bodice her shoulders rose like snow. A white rose nestled at her breasts. Her pale blond hair was caught in a low chignon at the nape of her neck.

She was the most beautiful woman Theo had ever seen. The most precious to him.

She stood looking at him, and his heart turned over.

'You've been kidnapped,' said Leandra to Theo Atrides. He stood stock still.

'Have I?' His voice husked.

'You're my prisoner,' she told him. Her words were a whisper. A promise.

He took a step towards her. Only one.

'On one condition,' he replied.

She shook her head, the light catching the beauty of her face. Her perfume reached him. He used all his self-control and stayed where he was.

'No conditions,' she told him. Her eyes were like glowing stars, answering the starlight as Venus glowed, hanging low in the sky. The goddess of love.

She was the goddess incarnate.

'One condition,' he repeated. Cruel. Harsh.

Her eyes widened unbearably, lips parting. Fearing what he would say.

'I want a life sentence,' said Theo Atrides to the woman he loved.

Her eyes were brighter than jewels. Brighter than stars. Bright with tears.

She gave a little choke. Such a little one. But he was there, the distance between them gone. Gone for ever.

He cradled her face in his hands. Long, and strong, and so absolutely tender.

'I love you, *thespinis*. I love you and I don't deserve you. But if you give me a second chance I will prove myself worthy of you if it takes all my life!'

She gazed up at him. The tears were still unshed, but hovered on her eyelashes. They were long and dusky. Not caked with mascara, the way they'd been when he'd first seen her. When he'd wanted to wipe off the layers of jarring make-up from her beautiful face and reveal the true loveliness beneath. She'd been the woman he would love even then, but he'd been too blind, too stupid, too arrogant to see it!

He saw it now.

'Can you forgive me, Leandra? Will you forgive me? Will you let me be your prisoner all my life?'

She shook her head.

'No,' she whispered. 'I will only let you be my lover.'

He smiled. A smile that lifted his haggard face and reached his eyes, his heart. Her heart.

'Oh, I am that—I am that for ever, Leandra. My Leandra. My lover and my love. My bride and my wife. The mother of my children. The jewel of my heart. My life. My heart. My eyes. My everything.'

She saw the tears gleam in his eyes. And drew him to her.

Later—an eternity later, an eyeblink later—after they had gone indoors, to where the fire burned in the grate and the iced champagne awaited them, after they had toasted Demos for his cunningly executed plan to bring them together, after *Antigone*'s brief run had finished, here on the island where they had first found happiness, and after Theo had led her through into the chilly bedroom and into the bed, which they warmed with their love until they both burned in the flames they had ignited in each other, then he held her to him, against his heart.

'How can you forgive me?' asked Theo Atrides, once so arrogant, now humbled by love. 'After everything I did to you—everything I said to you—'

Leandra smiled into his searching, doubting eyes, and told him the truth

'Because I love you,' she said, and the simple words were all he needed to hear, all she needed to say. A sly, teasing smile slid across her face. 'You see, Virgil also said, *"Omnia vincit amor,"'* she said softly. 'Shall I translate?'

A rueful look filled his eyes. *'Love conquers all.'*

'Very good,' she said approvingly, the teasing smile in her eyes now. 'You're not such a bad classics scholar yourself, Theo Atrides.'

The rueful look intensified.

'It's Demos who's the scholar in the family.'

'I know. He was an excellent coach—I could never have learnt *Antigone* without him!'

The rueful look changed to wonder—tinged with self-mocking chagrin.

'To my dying day I'll remember how I felt when I realised *Antigone* was you,' he said.

An unholy smile twitched at her lips. 'So will I,' she assured him. 'I have to confess, I was thinking pretty mean and nasty thoughts about you when I saw you sitting there next to Demos!' A questioning look clouded her eyes. 'Theo—about Demos…and Chris. Do you mind? I was so afraid you would. So were they.'

Theo stared at her uncomprehendingly. 'How can I possibly mind?' A glint entered his dark eye. 'You may think me an unreconstructed male chauvinist, *thespinis mou,*' he said baitingly, 'but knowing you have never slept with him fills me with deepest satisfaction! I was eaten with jealousy of him! And every time you praised him it was like a blow to me!'

'How will your grandfather react to Demos being gay?' she asked tentatively, her heart glowing with his possession.

'We have decided not to tell him just why he paraded you as his mistress to avoid marrying Sofia—there is little point now that he is so near death. Particularly now that she has become happily engaged to someone else.'

She smiled. 'I'm glad for her. I always felt sorry for her, waiting for Demos who could never marry her. But I hope Milo won't be too disappointed in losing a granddaughter-in-law.'

Theo's eyes gleamed. 'But he will be gaining one, *matia mou.* And such a one! Milo will be beside himself with joy. Not only is his obdurate, philandering older grandson finally doing his family duty and marrying, after he long ago washed his hands of me, but I am bringing home the perfect bride! Not only is she as beautiful as foam-born Aphrodite—' his hand tenderly caressed the soft roundness of her belly, where even now his seed was seeking its fruition '—not only is she eager to bear our child as soon as possible—' he kissed her gently, joyously, delighted that she had agreed to hasten the arrival of Milo's great-grandchild without delay '—but to crown her perfection she can spout Sophocles to him! She can even, I believe—' he smiled conspiratorially at her '—manage a little modern Greek as well, no? How fortunate,' he finished dryly, 'for your charade that Agathias and Yiorgos are deaf and you could not speak to them.'

He sobered, self-accusation in his eyes.

'It took me so long to realise you were not in any way the woman I took you for. Can you truly forgive me for being blinded by my own prejudices?'

It was Leandra's turn to look guilty.

'I held the truth back from you, Theo—in that I deceived you. I was trying to protect Demos—I couldn't break his confidence—he was so screwed up about telling you, in case you disowned him.'

'He and Chris love one another—and how can we, loving each other, condemn that?'

His generosity of spirit warmed her.

Then a frown creased the perfect happiness of her brow.

'Won't Milo mind, Theo—that I am the woman he thought was Demos's mistress?'

'Mind? He'll be insufferably pleased with himself. He sussed straight away I had been smitten with you! And since you're nothing like—'

He stopped.

She felt his sudden tension.

'Theo—?' Alarm was in her voice.

He held her against him, more tightly still.

Then, as if slowly releasing the poison that had long, long ago seeped into his bloodstream, he began to talk. She held him in the safety of her arms, the harbour where he now finally found shelter, and safety, and love.

'I was twenty-one,' he said slowly, staring sightlessly at the ceiling, memory taking him back down a bitter path. 'I was in Paris. Her name was Mireille. She was—' his mouth twisted '—a dancer in a nightclub. She was twenty-eight—

nearing the end of her career—but I never noticed that. She did, though. I was…besotted with her. I wanted to marry her. She told me she was pregnant. I phoned my parents that night and told them I was bringing home my bride. It was the happiest moment of my life.'

He stilled. His eyes looked out into the past.

'My father arrived in Paris the next day. Milo had sent him. My father paid Mireille three million dollars and took her to an abortion clinic. She went willingly. Then she flew to South America with her money. I never saw her again.' The baldness of his words could not hide the bleakness within. He took a short, tight breath, and went on.

'My father told me Mireille had confessed the child was not mine but another lover's—she had quite a few, he told me, all far more experienced than a twenty-one-year-old boy. He called the abortion—' his voice tightened unbearably '—a "minor complication". Between us all,' he said, his voice empty of all but bitterness and guilt, 'we created and killed an innocent child—whoever fathered him. To save the good Atrides name from unpleasant scandal.'

He paused. 'I vowed that day that never again would I be caught…or used…to create a child conceived purely because of someone's greed for the Atrides wealth. And that is why…that is why…' His voice choked.

She put her hand over his mouth. 'It's all right, Theo. It's all right. I understand now.' Her voice was very gentle.

He looked at her, turning his head so that her eyes looked into his, understanding all, forgiving all. He kissed her softly in gratitude.

Then not in gratitude at all.

As his kiss deepened his body hardened against hers.

'Pethi mou,' said Theo thickly, lifting his mouth momentarily from hers. 'I am crazy about you—just crazy, my sweet, enchanting Leandra!'

'I think it's mutual, Theo,' she moaned faintly, yielding her mouth to his again with an eager wantonness he found extremely arousing. Almost as arousing as he found it to

slide his body down alongside hers, his strong hands stroking her flanks as he positioned her to his satisfaction prior
to some serious lovemaking. As his kiss deepened his eyelids fluttered shut, long silky lashes splaying. In his loins
the engine of passion started to rev with pleasing precision.

'*Yineka mou,* but I want you again,' he murmured thickly,
not for the first time that evening—and certainly, he intended, not for the last. His lips moved to explore the tender
morsels of her earlobes.

This was a mistake, for it gave Leandra a chance to speak.
She knew they would never again need to speak of the
wound that had poisoned him so long ago, but there were
still two things preying on her peace of mind. She wanted
them banished for ever.

'Theo?'

He lifted his head, opening his eyes. There was a questioning look in hers, a note of anxiety in her voice. He
wanted to kiss it away from her. She must never look questioning or anxious again. He had hurt her so badly, but from
now on her life must be perfect in every detail. He, Theo
Atrides, would see to it. It would be his life's mission. The
prospect made him want to shout with joy and exultation.
He was the emperor of the world once more!

He moved to kiss her mouth again, but she drew back a
little from him, albeit with reluctance.

Theo stilled the swift burgeoning need in his body. His
own most beloved of women wanted to ask him a question.
He wanted to make love to her until she was breathless, but
in this, as in everything now, Leandra's needs must come
first.

'What is it, *thespinis mou?*' he said with great forbear-
ance.

That forbidden anxious look was still there. She bit her
lip. Theo wished she wouldn't. If anyone's teeth were going
to nip that tender flesh of hers they were going to be his!

'Theo,' she began diffidently, 'I...I may not have been
Demos's mistress, but I have...I have had other lovers,' she

finished in a rush. 'Two,' she admitted. 'One was at uni-versity—my first. We were, well, sort of experimenting. He was nice, but we broke up in the second year. The other was when I was on tour in rep. He was Darcy in a stage version of *Pride and Prejudice*. He looked a knock-out in knee breeches. But when the run was over I went off him terribly. That's all,' she said.

Theo received her confession with sublime unconcern.

'From now on there will be only me,' he informed her with happy possessiveness.

She grinned stupidly. The anxious look was gone. Theo never wanted it to come back.

'I think that will do for me,' she teased.

'Good,' he said, and decided it was definitely time to put this admirable policy into immediate practice. But as his hands slid up to shape her breasts, which they had been wanting to do for longer than was physically comfortable, she held him off again.

'And what about you? Does the same rule apply to you?'

He stared at her, outraged. 'Of course it does! Why should I want any woman but you? My beautiful white-breasted Aphrodite.'

He lowered his mouth purposefully to those very orbs. Leandra intercepted him and laid her fingers over his mouth.

'Theo?' she said for the third time.

Torture, thought Theo. That's what this is. He caught her fingers with his and kissed them lightly, before setting them aside to answer her.

'Yes, delight of my heart?' he answered, with gritted teeth and every muscle aching with self-control.

'What about Diana Delado?'

He stared at her blankly.

'Who?'

'Diana Delado?' repeated Leandra. 'You were all over the press with her!'

Theo grimaced at the note of accusation in her voice. Perhaps some ravishing lovemaking would improve her mood. His fingers made for the nearest nipple. She lifted his hand away.

'Won't one of the most beautiful and glamorous women in the world miss you accessorising her?' Leandra jibed. She was trying to sound brave about it, but Theo knew her soul now, and he heard the fear in her voice. Fear that his past would poison their future.

That must never happen. Theo lifted his weight back on to his elbow and gave an exaggerated sigh.

'Diana Delado,' he intoned patiently, 'is going to marry her senator, whose wife has filed for divorce in order to marry a twenty-six-year-old tennis pro. I merely diverted press attention until Diana could reveal her true intentions. We did not,' he said emphatically, gazing down at her, 'sleep together—I have touched no other woman since you, Leandra, and I never will again. There is only one woman I love, only one that I want, and by the grace of God, and her own forgiving heart, she is with me here, in my arms. And now, my own beloved, is there anything else you'd like to know?'

'Yes,' said Leandra. She was smiling now. Knowing that the man you loved could be so casually indifferent to one of the world's most beautiful and glamorous women was really very reassuring.

Theo Atrides held on fast to his self-control. This was the woman he loved. He had lost her through his own arrogant folly but she'd let him win her back. He would never do anything ever again to lose her—he would indulge her every whim. Even the ones that were driving him insane—like asking asinine questions at a time like this.

'What would you like to know, *thespinis mou?*' he enquired in a restrained, exquisitely courteous fashion.

'I'd like to know,' said Leandra, opening her eyes very wide and letting the tip of her tongue lick lightly at her lower lip, hooking her thigh over his and rubbing softly, while her hand wandered south again over his suddenly clenched abdominals until it reached its target, stroking it languorously with her finger, 'when you're finally going to get on with making love to me. You're keeping me waiting, Theo.' Her long eyelashes swept down, and then up again. 'And I don't like to wait,' she husked, with the most tempting smile playing on her lips, and a wicked, wicked light in her eyes, as her hand closed caressingly around him, feeling him jerk uncontrollably in her arousing grip and guiding him towards her own aching loins with growing urgency. 'I don't like to wait one little tiny bit, Theo darling...'

She didn't have to any longer. He fell on her like a starving man. She gave him the world, and heaven too.

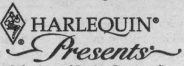

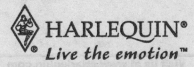

The world's bestselling romance series.

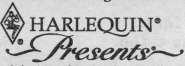

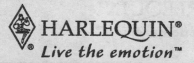

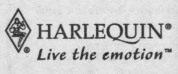

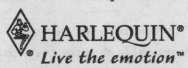